After Paris

Jacqueline Bacci

ISBN: 979-8-343-56883-7

After Paris

Copyright © 2024 Jacqueline Bacci

All rights reserved. No part of the book may be used or reproduced in any manner whatsoever without written permission.

Without limiting the author's exclusive rights any unauthorized use of this publication to train generative artificial intelligence (AI) technologies is expressly prohibited.

This is a work of fiction. Names, characters, places, and incidents are either the product of the author's imagination or are used fictitiously. Any resemblance to actual persons, living or dead, businesses, companies, events, or locales is entirely coincidental.

Kindly note that this book has scenes of grieving and childhood bereavement.

Cover by: Sidney at Hypography

DEDICATION

To my husband and son who always believed I could do anything I put my mind to, even when I did not.

Jacqueline Bacci

CHAPTER ONE

Paris

Alyssa

Watching the world go by whilst drinking a good cup of coffee is one of my favourite ever past times. Today I have surpassed even my own standards as today I am sitting outside a Parisian café, in the excitingly chic city of Paris itself and it is a beautiful spring day and the coffee is superb, just like you would expect. I am in my element. I may even be tempted to add a few of those scrumptious little 'petit pastries' they have inside the café to my order. I look at my mobile phone and grin to myself when I see it is raining in London today. I almost feel bad that I am instead enjoying the Parisian sunshine whilst my friends and family are at home in rainy old London town, almost but not quite.

I sat back in my chair and raised my coffee cup to my lips, taking in the wonderful aroma of the freshly ground coffee beans first before taking a gratifying sip. I closed my eyes in contentment and reveled in my good fortune. My life is finally getting back on track again and I would like to go as far as to say that it is the first time in a long time that I have felt happy. I am in Paris, the sun is shining, and I am finally doing what I love, I am writing my first novel and what better place to set my novel but Paris the city of love. I read somewhere once that Paris is the most visited city in the world and I, for one, could see the reason why. I have found an undeniable infinity with Paris with its 'chicness' and all its romantic qualities. Even in this cynical, technological age, Paris is still quintessentially old fashioned with its small boutiques and cafés, delicious food, majestic old buildings, and the savoir faire of the people who made it their duty to stop for lunch every day and catch up with their friends for what seems like hours on end. I supposed it was the French version of the Spanish siesta and the Italian 'dolce far niente' (the sweetness of doing nothing), part and parcel of the Parisian's daily routine. Sometimes I wonder if any Parisian ever really did any real work and how this whole bustling vibrant city managed to move ahead with the times but somehow it did.

Everywhere you look there seems to be couples in love, couples kissing, holding hands, embracing, unashamedly flirting. I had no end of muses for my novel and every day I found I scribbled something down in my notebook that I had seen or heard from the endless stream of lovers everywhere. I sighed and sipped my coffee and once again thought of how I was in a good place with my life at the moment. What did my best friend Naomi say the other day? We had video called each other and she had commented on how Parisian I looked with my new full fringe and my sophisticated new wardrobe, and I admitted I was learning from the women around me at every turn. She praised me and said that she thought that I was living my best life, and she was so nearly right, I almost was. I smiled to myself and took a moment to close my eyes, lifting my face up to the sun and basking in the warmth.

My quiet reverie did not last long. I heard her before I saw her. A barrage of long French words that I could not understand, and all said in rather a raised angry female voice. I opened my eyes and leant forward and saw that the voice belonged to a statuesque model-like blonde. She was dressed elegantly, as most women in Paris are, in a grey fitted trouser suit and it looked like she has nothing on underneath the jacket. It very quickly flitted across my mind that I wished I could wear something like that without having to wear a bra, but then my thoughts are taken back to the

After Paris

scene as I watched the French beauty turn to the man in her wake. I took another sip of coffee as they got nearer my table, her striding along with her long legs and he is following her trying what I can only assume to cajole her. At least that is what it seems to me. I strained my neck a bit to get a better look at the man and when I do I see what all the fuss is about.

He must be the most handsome man I have ever seen. He has dark hair that is longish and unruly, like he has just got out of bed and ran his fingers through it. There are very few people that can get away with that sort of look and this man is one of them. He is dressed in a suit that just had to be bespoke as it fits him so well and after all he is French...what more is there to say? His shirt is pristine and white and makes his lightly tanned skin look even more so. I watched his face as he takes a further onslaught of shouting from the blonde and detect a slight smile upon his full and luscious lips, even though from the tone of her voice and her body language towards him, she is not saying anything even mildly amusing. His eyebrows rose as she pointed a long-manicured finger at him, and he laughed. It is then I noticed his eyes. Blue. Turquoise blue, fringed with long dark lashes. He is perfect to look at but obviously he has done something seriously wrong to be on the receiving end of what I can only assume is abuse. They have now walked right in front of my table, and I surreptitiously watch the scene from behind my coffee cup, trying not to make eye contact with either of them.

Finally, he answered her back and his voice is deep and dark like chocolate velvet and the blonde stared at him for a long moment and then reached to my table, grabbed the salt cellar and threw it towards him. Unable to help myself I let out a gasp, momentarily stunned. What the hell has this man done? Luckily, it missed as he ducked, obviously accustomed to having things thrown at him by disgruntled beautiful women, and the small glass pot smashed on the cobblestones. The blonde angrily reached out to grab the matching pepper pot but this time he was too quick for her and caught her wrist in his hand. He said something to her, soft and low which I couldn't hear, and she glared at him with hot angry tears in her eyes and then wrenched her hand away and with a flick of her perfect blonde hair stalked away from him without even looking back. He watched her go with a look of what? Relief…pity…amusement? Well maybe a mixture of all three? And then his eyes met mine and my heart skipped a beat.

He said something to me in French, which of course I didn't understand but I smiled anyway.

"Luckily for you I'm English and didn't understand a word of what just happened."

"You look French," he said in a perfect English accent. "I was apologising for what you just had to witness."

I took a sip of my coffee and then placed the cup carefully back on its saucer. "Whatever you did must have been bad."

He smiled and shrugged his broad shoulders. "God, the French are so passionate. Passionate in love, anger, hate. They don't do half measures. Not like the cool reserved English. I must say I absolutely deserved it though."

"It's just fortunate I didn't need the salt," I observed looking over to the waiter cleaning up the mess from the pavement. "Excellent reflexes though."

"Rugby at school," he grinned. "I am actually quite proud that I still have the moves."

I couldn't help but smile back. "She was rather beautiful though. Model by any chance?"

"Yes," he answered with a smirk. "A rather spoilt one too. I really must learn my lesson when it comes to women who are used to getting their own way most of the time. I seem to be a glutton for punishment." He pulled out the chair opposite me. "May I?"

I shrugged and ignored my heart beating just that little bit faster at the nearness of him. "Please do."

A waiter appeared from inside the café and my 'much-too-handsome-for-his-own-good' companion ordered a coffee and looked at me. "Can I offer you a fresh coffee? It's the least I can do after ruining your peace and quiet."

"Thanks. I will have the same again please."

The waiter nodded and left to fulfil our order.

"So, what brings you to Paris?" He asked leaning back in his chair to study me a little too intently. I felt my cheeks colour and took a deep breath.

"Research," I said forcing a confident smile to my lips.

After Paris

"For what? Are you some sort of scientist? A chemist perhaps?" He raised an eyebrow and grinned.

"I am working on secret formula for the UK Government. It is based on how French women eat so much wonderful food all the time and manage to stay so slim and sexy leaving the rest of us with no chance whatsoever."

He laughed and then looked at me for a long moment until I looked away embarrassed and pretended to look at some lady walking past with a poodle under her arm sporting a huge pink bow in its hair.

"So really what's the research for?"

"Something entirely less interesting, which is my book. I am a writer."

He smiled and raised both eyebrows at that. "Wow. What kind of books do you write?"

The waiter came and brought our coffees. The smell was divine. I took a deep breath. "You ask a lot of questions."

"Well, it's because I feel like I am on the back foot. You learned a lot about me by the scene played out in front of you earlier."

"I don't speak French and so I had no idea what was being said."

"But you got the gist, being a writer, it must help you read people."

"Yes, I am good at reading situations and people," I agreed.

"So, tell me. What did you think was happening earlier between me and Madeleine?"

Madeleine. What else would that perfect specimen of womankind have been called?

"You were having a lover's tiff. She caught you flirting with another woman, or maybe worse? She thought she was the only woman in your life or at the very least wanted to be the only woman in your life and she was jealous and angry and gave you an ultimatum. You told her that you could never promise her what she wants and then the whole salt cellar throwing incident," I looked at his amused face as he sipped his coffee. "Am I near?"

I watched as he put down his coffee and leant towards me holding out his hand. "I'm Xavier."

Of course you are. Even his name was sexy and French and if anyone was going to be called Xavier it would be him. I put my

hand in his and felt the tingle go from my wrist right through my body…my whole body. I tried to ignore the feeling and smiled.
"Alyssa."
We stared at each other, my hand still in his until I snapped out of my trance and pulled my hand away immediately picking up my coffee and taking a long sip as I studied him.
"Well?" I asked.
"Well, what?"
"Was I near with my observations?"
He smiled. "I will tell you tonight over dinner."
Very smooth…too smooth. This man was used to getting what he wanted. Unfortunately, not this time.
I shook my head with more than a tinge of regret.
"I can't come to dinner with you."
"What?? I get condiments thrown at me and then turned down for dinner all in the same day?" he grinned. "Come on. Come to dinner."
It was tempting…so very tempting but he was bound to trouble with a capital T, and I did not need any more complications in my life. I shook my head.
"Sorry. I am working. That's why I came to Paris. For work."
Not entirely true, but all he needed to know for now.
"Thought you came to do research? A night on the town with me would be great research."
I bit my lip to stop the laugh bubbling in my throat. "Not the kind of research I came for unfortunately."
"Mademoiselle, you wound me." He placed both hands over his heart and closed his eyes.
"Do you live here in Paris?" I asked, again trying not to laugh.
"Come to dinner and I will tell you all."
I shook my head and stood up. I had to leave before I gave in.
"Xavier. It was lovely to meet you and I especially loved the lover's tiff. It made my day so much more entertaining than I could have imagined."
His eyebrows rose at that one and he grinned.
"So glad I could at least entertain you, which means my day has not been a complete disaster," He pulled a card out of the breast pocket of his immaculate suit and held it out to me. "Just in case

After Paris

you change your mind at any point - in the name of research of course."

I took it from his long slim suntanned fingers, careful not to touch him again. He was lethal. Our eyes held as I took the card without looking at it and slipped it into my pocket.

"Au revoir."

He didn't answer just smiled and slightly bowed his head and when I discreetly looked back from the corner of the street, he was still watching me and, secretly pleased, I had to smile.

I felt as light as a feather as I walked along in the spring sunshine. My fingers went to the card in my pocket, and I pulled it out taking in the thick richness of the cream card and the gold embossed writing. Even his business card was sexy.

Xavier Montgomery
The Montgomery Corporation
Paris. London. Madrid.

On the back was his phone number in all three places. I smiled and put it back into my pocket. Maybe I would call him. There was something about him that made me want to find out if he had felt it too, that undefinable thing that pulled us towards each other. We had spoken for a few moments, a few moments out of a lifetime and yet I knew that it would not be the last time we would see each other.

Xavier

Fuck. Today had been a complete nightmare. Could it get any worse?

I sat at my desk and looked out of the window with the Eiffel Tower in the background, a view that usually pleased me to no end, but today it just was a view. The only bright spot in my day had been meeting Alyssa. I leaned back in my chair and stretched out my legs and thought about her. I think I am losing my appeal. She categorically turned me down for dinner which was almost unheard of. *Xavier Montgomery, you are losing it.*

I picked up my mobile just to see if there were any messages. Six from Madeleine, two from some girl called Rosalie, who I couldn't even remember meeting, and four from my Mum. None from Alyssa. Crisis talks were needed. I speed dialed one of my best friends Eduardo, a lawyer at some fancy firm in London.

"Hey!" he answered almost straight away. "How did it go with Madeleine?"

"Madeleine who?" I deadpanned.

He laughed. "You told her then? That it was over? How did she take it?"

"Swimmingly of course. It's history. But I did get bombarded with condiments," I closed my eyes at the raucous laughter that greeted me from down the phone.

"What the fuck?" Eduardo laughed. "You French and your gastronomy. Even your break ups involve food!"

"Thanks for your understanding you little piece of *merde*. These French women do my head in. I should have cut her off weeks ago."

"As I told you," Eduardo replied just a little smugly. "But no. You couldn't resist. You had to go and fuck her best friend too, at the same time, for weeks."

"It was a moment of weakness. Lilly worked at the Moulin Rouge, and you know I can never resist a dancer's supple and flexible body. The things she could do with that body…" I added wistfully.

"Spare me the details you degenerate; you were playing with fire, and you knew that eventually your fingers were going to get well and truly burnt."

"Yeah, well now they are both off the scene and I find myself alone and single and in Paris. What is a guy to do?"

"Keep your dick in your pants for once?" Eduardo suggested and ignoring my snort of laughter he carried on. "Just try and act like a grown man of thirty-four and not some hormonal adolescent."

I snorted a laugh again. "Yeah right. Next?"

"You could pay a visit to that club I was telling you about…Masquerade…the one my client owns there in Paris."

"Ed, I am not into sex clubs. How many times do I have to tell you? All that kinky shit does not rock my boat."

"Listen, this club is not like that. I mean it is if you want it to be.

After Paris

But it is class. The women are perfect, and they will do whatever you ask. If you are not into kink that's fine, vanilla is also on the menu."
"Never said I was vanilla, maybe vanilla with chocolate sauce and some sprinkles."
"Yes, shut up. You are making me nauseous. Want me to ring my client and get you a private room? It usually costs a fortune, but he owes me."
I pondered it over in my mind. What I really wanted was for the delectable Alyssa to call me and go out to dinner with me. I should have been more forceful; I should have asked for her number. I should have at least asked where she was staying. All that dramatic shit with Madeleine had thrown me off my game. There had been a connection between us. I had felt it, and I knew she felt it too by how she has reacted towards me. There was an underlying sexual tension, but I was reeling from my encounter with the French banshee and found it hard to rein it in. Alyssa had been beautiful. Beautiful and desirable. Now, who knew if I would ever see her again?
"Yes. Call him. Let me know. I have had a shit day. It can't get any worse right?"
"Oh no Xavier, your day is going to get a whole lot better believe me. You will be thanking me tomorrow."
"Have you ever been there?"
"Xavier, I have a membership."
"You never told me."
"Not really something you talk about. Plus, the whole thing is top secret. You never speak about it afterwards."
"Shit! You're scaring me now. What are you getting me into?" I stood up and walked over to my window and stared out at bustling Paris below. It was a beautiful city but like any city it had its dark side too, one that I had never really explored before.
"Don't be such a chicken. You need to get more sophisticated with your sex life and stop fucking dance girls and models. I will leave your name at the door. You will go by the name Casanova."
I laughed. "You're shitting me, right?"
"No. Casanova. Rather fitting I think."
I sighed. "Fine, Casanova. Whatever."

"Enjoy."

A package was waiting for me with the concierge at my apartment building when I got home. It was in a plain black glossy flat box. Inside there was a black mask and a white card with the name 'Masquerade' discreetly in the corner in black font. There was message typed on the card.

Your appointment is at 10pm. We look forward to your visit Mr. Casanova. Please wear the mask.

Holy Shit. This has just got real, and it looked like I was going to a sex club tonight.

CHAPTER TWO

Xavier

At 9.55pm I was dressed in an evening suit and standing outside the very discreet black front door of the Masquerade club. A text had come through on my phone giving me the address and I had my driver take me there. There was a buzzer on the door just with an image of a mask. It reminded me to put my own one on and I did so, tying it tightly at the back of my head - wouldn't want it falling off.
I rang the buzzer. The door clicked open, and I entered. The inside was surprisingly classy and not dark and dingy like I imagined it would be. It was light with white marble floors and walls and black accessories such as the doors and mirrors. A woman approached me. She was dressed in slinky black evening gown and wore a mask. Her skin was pale, and her hair was blonde and long almost down to her curvy arse. I could feel the excitement building. If the women were all like her, I could tell I was going to be in for a very entertaining evening.
"Good evening, Mr. Casanova," she smiled, her red lipstick looking even more vibrant against her white even teeth. "Would you follow me please?"
I followed her down the corridor to set of black glossy double doors. She reached out and swung them open and politely stood back gesturing for me to enter and then she closed the doors

behind me.

A man, in a mask of course, sat behind a huge black desk. He smiled. "Please take a seat Mr. Casanova. Just a few rules and regulations before you enter Masquerade."

"Of course," I answered and took a seat opposite him.

"You have come to the club on a recommendation, and we are really pleased to welcome you. However, there are some very strict rules that we abide by here. Are you ok for me to list these to you?"

I nodded.

"Good. Firstly, we need to get you to sign a confidentiality clause please. We do not discuss what happens in the club outside of these walls," he slid a piece of paper across the desk to me and as I cast my eyes over the details he carried on. "The women here choose who they want to spend the night with. You do not approach the women. Is that understood?"

I looked up from the paper at him. "What if I don't wish to be with that woman?"

"They will approach you and whisper in your ear yes or no and it is then you have the choice. If you say no the woman will walk away and if you say yes, the woman will lead you to a private room where she will be yours for the night."

I nodded. "Ok. That seems fair."

"Mr. Casanova you will see things in this club that you will not see anywhere else. Anything you see is on a total voyeuristic level. You do not join in. They are there for your viewing pleasure only."

What the fuck?

"Anything you see that you like, just mention this to your chosen lady and she will arrange it for you in the privacy of your room or in a viewing room if you would prefer."

I held out my hand to take the Mont Blanc pen being offered to me for signing and signed my name with a flourish, pushing both the pen and the paper back to him. "Viewing room?"

"Where other guests can watch the proceedings."

I cleared my throat. *Fuck.* That wasn't happening. I wasn't having people watch me doing anything to anyone.

"That concludes our business. I will call Serena back to take you

After Paris

into the club. Have a good night, Mr. Casanova."
I heard the doors open behind me and there she was. The blonde. I stood up and followed her down the corridor. We stopped in huge lobby where there were another set of magnificently carved black doors. She typed in a code and the doors swung open.

"Enjoy," she whispered in my ear.

Inside it was darker. It took my eyes a minute or so to adjust. There was soft sexy background music and for a moment it looked like any other club. But then the first thing I saw was a couple on a plinth lit up with purple light. They were both naked and were kissing and caressing each other's bodies. I moved on and saw another couple having sex on a huge sofa as others stood around and watched. Holy shit! What the hell has Eduardo got me into? I mean I had watched a bit of porn in my time, but this was taking it to a whole different level.

I walked on feeling kind of strange watching other people having sex. A hostess passed by and offered me a glass of champagne which I gladly took as my throat had suddenly dried up for some reason. I took a huge gulp and let my eyes wander around. There was a crowd around a stage that was lit up in red. I weaved in and out of the crowd until I could see what they were looking at. It was a beautiful girl naked in the middle and her arms and legs were tied at the top and the bottom so that she was spread eagled in an x shape. Three very fit muscular men were around her naked too, one of them was licking her breasts, one was having sex with her from behind and the other was watching as he stroked himself. Despite everything that was wrong with that scenario in my head I felt turned on and my cock jerked in my trousers. I took another gulp of my champagne, and it was then I saw her. Dressed in a black evening dress, dark shiny hair to her shoulders and her eyes seemingly mesmerised by what she was watching on the stage. She instantly reminded me of the girl from the café Alyssa, and straight away I was interested but shit! I couldn't approach her.

I watched her from across the stage as she watched the proceedings. She bit her lip as if she was trying to pull herself away, trying to distance herself from what was happening.

I wove through the crowd trying to get nearer to her and just as

I was nearly there a gentle hand touched my arm. I turned. She was blonde and beautiful and dressed in a black figure-hugging dress that left nothing to the imagination.

"Yes, or no?" she whispered in my ear.

My eyes darted to the brunette who was now watching me and the blonde with interest. Something connected between us, and I turned to the blonde.

"No…thanks."

She smiled and nodded her head and disappeared back into the crowd. I turned to the brunette again but in that split second, she had gone. My eyes darted around looking for her but nothing. Then I heard a soft voice in my ear.

"Yes, or no?"

I turned around and there she was. She was breath taking. Slim but curvaceous at the same time with big breasts and a tiny waist, she was beautiful. Her dress was demure compared to some of the others I had seen, but somehow that made it sexier.

"Yes," I whispered back against her hair that smelled like citrus fruits.

She smiled and took my hand and led me away from the crowds and out of the main room and up some stairs until she stopped outside a door. She tapped in a code and the door swung open. She led the way, and I watched her curvy arse as she sashayed over to the bed and turned to face me as I closed the door behind us.

We stared at each other in silence.

"What made you choose me?" she asked. She had an English accent just like Alyssa today and immediately I was glad she had picked me.

"You remind me of someone."

I heard her slight intake of breath as she watched me carefully.

"You remind me of someone too."

"English?" I asked taking a step nearer.

She nodded. "Disappointed?"

I shook my head. "Definitely not. I am half English myself."

"Thought you may prefer a French woman?"

"Had enough of French women to last me a lifetime," I smiled.

A slight smile played around her delectable lips. "So, what is it

After Paris

that you are looking for tonight?"
I took a deep breath. What the hell does someone say to that?
"I don't know. Let's just see how things go shall we?"
"Ok…" she hesitated.
"What?" I asked.
"Do you want a viewing room?"
I snorted a laugh. "Definitely not! Sex for me is private and personal."
"And yet you have come to a sex club…?"
"Yeah…it's a long story."
I walked nearer to her, and she immediately tensed. I could see it in her body and the limited view I had of her eyes through the mask. I stopped and she smiled.
"Sorry. I am a tad nervous. I have never done this before…"
To say I was surprised was putting it mildly. If she was telling the truth, part of me was glad that this woman standing before me had never been with anyone else inside this club.
"So, this is your first night?"
"Actually, it's my one and only night here."
"What are you on job share?" I asked with a laugh.
She grinned. "Yes. Something like that. Seriously, if you want me to call the blonde that showed interest in you, I can go and find her…."
"No!" I interrupted her a bit more harshly than I intended. I took a deep breath. "I want you."
"Even though I am new to this?"
I smiled. "So am I. Turns out this is my first time too. So, let's learn together, ok?"
She nodded. "Ok."
She stepped towards me and stared into my eyes. Shit, why does she seem so familiar? Her fingers went to my silk bow tie, and she pulled it undone and then she undid the buttons on my shirt starting at the top, her fingertips skimming over every bit of flesh that was slowly revealed. I literally trembled under her touch.
She was so intoxicating, and the masks made it sexy and decadent and mysterious. She pulled my shirt from my trousers and pushed it off my shoulders. I undid the cufflinks and shrugged my shirt off. Her eyes appraised my chest as she traced a fingertip from

my throat down to just above the waistband of my trousers. I was hard as a rock. I laughed softly.

"You sure you've never done this before?"

She smiled. "Oh, yes I've done *this* before…just not here at this club with a stranger."

Her words aroused me.

"I wanted to fuck you the first moment I saw you," my voice was deep and full of my desire for her. She licked her lips and stared at me.

"I know," she whispered. We stared at each other for a long moment.

"Take your dress off," I whispered to her.

Her hands moved to the straps of her dress, and she pushed them from her slim shoulders. They slid down her arms and then it seemed that her dress seemed to fall in one heavy movement to down around her ankles. She stepped out and kicked it to one side with her high black fuck-me shoes. Underneath she wore a black lacy corset and fuck, she had on stockings and suspenders with her creamy soft thighs visible at the tops. I had died and gone to heaven. This woman was killing me. Her breasts were large and full and brimming over the top of the bodice and her waist was small pulled in the constraints of the corset which in turn made her hips round and lush and womanly.

"Turn around," I said. My voice had turned husky with need for this woman.

She turned full circle giving me a great view of her soft peachy backside over the top of those stockings. I almost came just from looking at her.

"Like what you see?" she asked as she turned to face me again.

I nodded. I didn't want to talk anymore. I just wanted her.

She held her head to one side and said softly "Can I ask you something…did that scene outside turn you on?"

"The last one? The woman with the three men?" I asked visualising it on my head. "Yes. Surprisingly it did."

"Me too," she smiled. "I have never seen anything like that before."

"So, we were both turned on. Just how wet were you watching that?"

After Paris

"Embarrassingly so."

"I want to feel how wet you are," I whispered.

We stared hard at each other as I moved closer and gently pulled her black lacy thong to one side. I could already feel how wet she was by the lace of her panties in my hand. I stroked between her legs, and she moaned softly. Fuck! She was soaking. I groaned loudly and rubbed my fingertips hard over her clit. She moaned again and bucked against my hand. She looked at my mouth and that just finished me. I had to kiss her. I pulled her to me and kissed her hard and demanding, pushing my tongue into her mouth and taking all she had. She tasted like honey, and I couldn't pull away from her. She was kissing me back, running her hands through my hair at the nape of my neck and pushing her gorgeous body against mine. My hand was still on her sex, and I loved the way she writhed against me.

I pulled my hand away and her eyes flew open in protest. I was being selfish I knew but I just needed to fuck her. I tore her panties from her body, and she gasped and then I turned her around and pushed her to the nearest wall where I pushed her arms above her head, her hands splayed on the wall, and she bent her forward so that I could look at her peachy naked backside. It was perfect. One hand stroked between her legs as the other pulled at my belt and my trousers and finally shoes and my socks until I was only in my boxers and my mask.

"Stay there," I said as I grabbed a condom from the assortment in a glass bowl on the bedside table. "And spread your legs."

I heard her gasp, but she did as she was told. She spread her legs wide, and I couldn't put the condom on quickly enough. For some reason Alyssa's face flashed fleetingly through my mind but I tried to dispel it as I looked at the woman waiting in anticipation for me spread eagled against the wall.

CHAPTER THREE

Alyssa

I never had any intention of joining in with any of the activities in Masquerade. My editor had gone through extreme lengths and managed to get me special permission to enter for one night only. It turned out she had been the best friend of the owner's wife at school. I had stipulations, of course I had. I couldn't name the club and wasn't allowed to even say which city it was in. My visit was purely for me on a personal basis to experience the atmosphere of the club and what happened there. I had also to dress like one of the hostesses. The owner assured me that the women of Masquerade approached the men, not the other way around and so I was safe. At least I thought I was. Until I saw him. Xavier. I knew it was him straight away. The masks were good, but they couldn't hide his confident sex appeal and his intense stare. I had been watching three men and a girl and strangely enough until that moment I had watched the 'entertainment' with a detached journalist's eye but the minute I saw Xavier everything changed. His nearness brought all my sensual feelings to the surface, and I started to imagine that it was me up there on that plinth and that he was with me, doing all those things to me. I saw the stunning blonde approach him and for a moment I thought he was going to accept her. He liked blondes after all. I had good evidence of that, but he had locked

After Paris

eyes with me across the room and I saw him subtly shake his head after she had whispered in his ear. The owner had said that of course I was free to choose a man too, if I felt so inclined, but at the time I had balked at the idea. Having sex with strangers was way out of my remit, even for the job I lived for and loved. But of course, Xavier was not a total stranger, and I could not deny the pull I had towards him earlier in the day. I decided to throw caution to the wind and approach him.

As I whispered Yes or No in his ear, I caught the smell of him and felt my stomach lurch with longing. God, he smelt so good, and he looked so heart wrenchingly handsome in his evening suit that I couldn't wait to get him alone in a room. I did wonder if perhaps he had recognised me too, but it seemed not although when he said I reminded him of someone I thought I had been caught. But so far so good. I must admit my mask covered more of my face than his did. It was half mask down to my nose whereas his was just covering his eyes. Not enough though...the turquoise of his eyes burned into mine whenever we spoke, and I found that I just couldn't look away.

Now here I was half naked and spread open to him up against a wall. It was so exciting and exhilarating and I just knew as soon as he touched me, I was going to be undone.
I looked over my shoulder as he walked towards me now naked. His body was perfection, muscly but not too much, broad shoulders, abs, flat stomach, slim hips, and strong thighs tapering down into long slim legs. His cock was huge and hard, jutting up and out against his flat stomach. He had donned a condom, and I closed my eyes in anticipation. Should I tell him...tell him who I am? It was forbidden and strictly against club policy but then I wasn't really working here.
His hand trailed across my back, and I actually trembled. His fingertips traced the blue butterfly tattoo on my shoulder.
"Symbolic of something?" he asked. "Or a drunken mistake?"
"Symbolic," I whispered back. "To me it means freedom, being able to finally spread my wings and fly. Butterflies also symbolise new beginnings."
"Wow..." he whispered as his hands went to my waist and then

caressed my naked buttocks. "That sounds intriguing…I sense there is a story behind those words."

"Yes," I breathed as his hands travelled over my skin leaving a trail of goose bumps in their wake. "But not for here and now. There are more important things to address…" My words trailed off as he touched the very core of me with his fingers and I jolted.

"You are so very beautiful," he whispered against my ear. "So desirable…just so…" He inserted two fingers inside me, and I moaned softly.

"Fuck…." The obscenity came out of his mouth as almost a caress as I pushed back against his hand.

"You need to fuck me," I whispered. "I need you to."

He kissed my neck softly and then kissed my tattoo.

"Happy to oblige," he whispered huskily.

He withdrew his fingers and positioned the tip of his cock between my legs and nudged gently at my opening. I strained back against him. I wanted him inside me so much. His hands went to my hips, and he held on as with one hard thrust, he filled me. I moaned out loud. It had been so long since I had felt a man inside me. Xavier was the man to blow all those cobwebs away. He was just like I had imagined he would be, forceful and yet highly skilled. This man knew what he was doing, and I suddenly hated all the women he had had before and all those that would come after me. He pulled out and plunged back in and it felt so good…he felt so good. I could hear his soft groans as he moved inside me moving his hips back and forth until I cried out.

He stopped and pulled me close for a moment. "Are you ok?" His lips were on my neck as he nuzzled in that place between my neck and my shoulder.

"Yes," I answered my voice low and husky. "Please don't stop…"

I felt his smile against my neck as he began to thrust again this time a bit harder and with a bit more force. I was so near the edge. I felt my orgasm building inside me. My groans became more urgent, my movements more out of control and then suddenly I was bucking against him as it hit me like a tsunami. Wave after wave of pure pleasure took over my body and Xavier held me close as I let it ride over me, unable to stop it even if I

After Paris

had wanted to. I heard his husky groans behind me as he began to thrust into me again, he was losing control himself and I still pulsed around him as he let go, moaning into my neck as his orgasm finally burst from his body.

Both of us were breathing like we had just run a marathon. His arms were still around me; he was still inside me, and I wasn't sure that I wanted him to move…not ever.

He laughed softly. "Shit…that was…"

"Amazing?" I supplied my voice still a bit breathless.

"Yes," he kissed my shoulder. "Are you sure you don't work here?"

"I do tonight…."

"What happens now?" he asked as he gently pulled out of me causing us both to let out a quiet gasp.

"Whatever you want," I swallowed the feeling of disappointment enveloping me at the thought he may want to sample other things that were on offer. "If you want to go back in the room and find another hostess?"

I watched as he disposed of the condom and then turned to stare at me. "What? Why would I do that? I want you."

I breathed a sigh of relief. "Of course. That is your prerogative."

He grinned. "That's what I want. You…all night long…but more than that I want you out of that corset right now."

I laughed and turned around. "You'll need to help me."

Those long slim fingers of his began to deftly untie the laces at the back of the very intricate corset that I had bought earlier at a charming little lingerie shop down one of the back streets. It had been an absolute jewel box of a shop with such delicate and provocative beautiful lingerie, that I had found myself spoilt for choice. But this one had just screamed intimacy and clandestine affairs.

"You are quite an expert," I smiled as gradually the black lace fell away from my body and I felt myself able to breathe again.

"Hardly surprising. I've lived in Paris for the past three years and French women seem to wear these as matter of course."

I giggled. "Yes well, they would. They are sexy without even trying too hard. I kind of hate them and idolise them all at the same time."

I felt the last clip and ribbon give way and my breasts fell free and Xavier held the exquisite and very expensive under garment in his hands for a fleeting moment before it fell from his fingertips to the floor.

I didn't move. Just stood perfectly still as I felt his intense gaze take in my now very exposed body clad only in stockings, suspenders, and high heeled pumps.

"The French have nothing on you," he whispered close to my ear. I closed my eyes as I felt his fingertips trail down my spine and my back arched involuntarily at his touch. His hands caressed my buttocks, and I heard his intake of breath as they gradually slid across my hips to my stomach. I moaned softly as they travelled upwards, skimming my rib cage, and finally cupping my breasts, his thumbs brushing across my tight bud nipples which hardened even more from his touch.

"First pair of full real breasts I have felt in three years," he whispered gruffly in my ear. "They are magnificent."

He cupped them in his hands, squeezing my flesh softly, and tweaking my nipples between his fingertips. It was pleasure and pain all at once and I could feel myself disintegrating beneath those wonderful hands of his. His hands travelled to my shoulders, and he pulled me around to face him. His eyes went from my breasts to my face, and I felt myself drowning in the want and need that I saw in those deep turquoise blue pools of lust.

He lowered his head and with a soft groan he took one nipple between his lips and suckled. I threw back my head and let out a long sigh. His hands and his mouth were made for my body. Everything and everyone that had gone before paled into insignificance as he sucked and bit and licked his way into my memory forever. No one would ever be able to make me feel as he was making me feel this night, this one night, in Paris. Because that was all it could ever be.

As that thought flitted through my mind, he pulled his lips from my breast and looked up at me. "Are you, ok?"

I nodded not trusting myself to speak.

"I felt your body tense," he said softly. "Anything you don't want me to do…just tell me…"

After Paris

How could he have felt what I was feeling? It was true, I felt a connection to him, a connection that I had never felt with anyone ever, but was he also attuned to me? Was it possible that he felt the same? It couldn't be. He had womaniser written all over him, even the first time I saw him he was breaking up with a beautiful model. I was reading way too much into this. He couldn't feel the same.

Let it go Alyssa...just enjoy this...enjoy him...
I shook my head vehemently. "Everything you are doing is.... amazing."

He grinned and another little piece of my heart fell into oblivion. He lowered his mouth again, but his eyes held mine as he sucked again on my nipple. I watched him as he gave himself to the moment and closed his eyes as he moaned against my flesh. Then he withdrew and stood up to his full height and his lips were crashing down on mine and he delved deep with his mouth and his tongue as he pulled me towards him crushing me against his lean hard body. He was relentless and I kissed him back with all I had wanting him to have all of me, wanting him to take all I had to give and wanting him to always think of Paris and to remember me. Then he picked me up in his arms and carried me to the awaiting bed.

Xavier

As I sank into her soft folds I knew, I just knew that this was not just some mindless fuck with a stranger. I looked down at her writhing beneath me, her perfect body moving in time with mine, the same rhythm, the same want, and the same need. I closed my eyes as I plunged inside her, her softness met my hardness, and it was like it was just meant to be. She was the Eve to my Adam, the Juliet to my Romeo the.... what am I thinking? I opened my eyes again and looked at her. She was looking up into my face and for a split second I saw something in her eyes, something more than just carnal pleasure, something deeper, more valid. I wanted to see her face. Her whole face not just those deep, dark, bottomless pools of her eyes. I reached forward to lift her mask,

but she stopped me, gripping my wrist with a strength I would not have thought she possessed.
"Against the rules," she whispered huskily.
"I need to see you," I whispered back. "I want to see your face..."
"I can't..." she took my face in her hands and pulled me down for a kiss. It was deep and full of longing. "Please understand."
"But you don't really work here," I pulled my head back to look at her.
"But I do tonight. My instructions were very clear. No names. No faces. Anonymity."
"So, I can fuck you senseless without knowing your name or seeing your face...that's ok, is it?" My words were brutal but for some reason I suddenly felt hurt and totally out of my comfort zone. I was usually so into this kind of sex...sex without boundaries...sex in its purest form without any ties and commitments, but not here and now and not with this beautiful woman. Shit. Her eyes stared up at me and there was more than a hint of sadness there. Fuck, now I had hurt her.
"Sorry," I muttered but I wasn't. Not really. Only sorry that I had hurt her with my words not sorry for how I was feeling.
"Would it help if I told you that this is special for me? I don't...I mean I had no intention of having sex with anyone tonight...and then I saw you," She smiled up at me. "I wanted you the moment I saw you and it has nothing to do with this place."
I mulled her words over in my mind and let out a deep breath that I wasn't aware I was holding.
"I don't know why this is bothering me. This is like a dream. No commitment sex I should be in my element right now."
She reached up and softly traced a red manicured fingertip down my cheek and across my jawline. "So be in your element. Make me remember this night forever."
Despite how I felt, her words still managed to turn me on, and I felt my already hard cock become even harder inside her. She moaned softly and closed her eyes. I slid my hands down her arms and entwined her fingers with my own and pulled her arms up roughly above her head, holding her prisoner beneath me. Her soft curvaceous body was now taut and pulled tight against mine.

After Paris

Her full breasts against my chest, her hips aligned with mine and our bodies joined together as intimately as they could be. I began to move inside her, slowly and deeply, looking into her eyes as I held her hands captive. Her breathing became laboured and heavy, and her lips parted to let out soft moans each time my cock went deep inside her. God, she felt like heaven. I gently let go of her hands, but she kept them above her head pushing against the cream velvet headboard as I maneuvered my hands behind her knees instead and held her thighs wide apart as I pistoned into her, losing all sense of reason and of gentleness. I just wanted to fuck her hard, tip her over the edge, fuck her so that she ached between her legs for days afterwards and with each move she would remember me. If there was only ever going to be this night, I wanted to ruin her for any other man that came after me. At that thought, a wave of jealously washed over me and I lost control. Her head was tipped back against the pillows as she met every one of my hard thrusts with one of her own. She was close, so close to orgasm. Her thighs were shaking, and her movements had become erratic, but I did not hold back. I wanted to see her let go, see her surrender to me and see her become undone because of me. It started slowly but she gripped the sheets with her fingers, her knuckles turning white and then her moans became louder, and her hips thrashed beneath mine as she cried out and finally let go. Her body pulsed around mine as she gave in to it and as I watched her convulse, she looked wild and beautiful, and it all became too much for me. I threw back my head as my orgasm ripped through my body and I could not stop the loud almost animalistic moans that escaped my lips as my hot seed spurted from my body. It seemed to go on forever and I knew that I had never come so hard not with any other woman. I suddenly lost the strength in my arms, and I crashed down against her body, burying my head in her neck as she clung to me and somewhere in my subconscious it became apparent that I would never forget her sweetly yielding body for the rest of my life.

When I awoke some hours later it was still dark outside, but she was gone. On the pillow next to me was her mask.

CHAPTER FOUR

London

Alyssa

I knocked on Harriet's door and heard her bark "Come in," in her usual dulcet tones. I poked my head around the door.
"You wanted to see me?"
She looked up from her screen and beamed. "Ah Alyssa. Yes. Come in and close the door."
I looked behind her to the view. It was a spectacular view of the river Thames and all the famous landmarks along its winding path, and it looked especially surreal today as the sun was shining and old London town looked beyond breath taking.
"Did I mention to you that if you ever decide to give up your office, I will happily take it off your hands?" I asked as I sat down opposite her.
She raised her eyebrows. "That view gets boring," she deadpanned.
"Yeah right," I grinned. "That view could never get boring."
"And neither does your writing. Well done on the latest interview, both insightful and deep. I loved every word of it and so I have a new assignment for you."
I rolled my eyes. "I guessed you might have. You know I am

trying to finish my book don't you…?"
She waved her hand in the air like she was swatting some insistent insect. "Yes, I know, some kind of flaky romantic airy-fairy stuff. You said already."
Harriet Carmichael was a hardnosed journalist and thought anything written outside of intense ground-breaking investigative journalism a waste of time.
"Harri, it's not easy writing romance. It's hard and I have a deadline."
"So, a lovely five figure sum to booster your flagging romance writer bank balance won't sway you huh?"
She had my attention. "What?"
She smiled with self-satisfaction and sat back in her chair. "One man, two weeks, copy on my desk in three weeks equals money in the bank."
"What man?" I asked leaning forward my interest piqued.
"A rich powerful banker with an aristocratic family and with so many skeletons in his closet that I can hear their bones rattling from here…"
"What's the angle? His work or his past?" I leaned forward trying not to formulate the idea of how I was going to construct this interview which was already whirling around in my head.
"Both. His father was a diplomat, his mother a French film star. He is currently the hottest thing in London. I am guessing he is a womaniser of the first degree and making more money per second than anyone else in the stock market. He has just transferred here from his Paris office and already he has been in the news more times than you could wave a stick at. Doesn't hurt that he is easy on the eye too, if you like that film star slash rakish kind of thing."
I snorted a laugh. "What? Like you don't?" My stomach had flipped at the mention of Paris, but I knew I was being paranoid. *Forget Paris Alyssa…*
Harriet raised an eyebrow. "A bit too pretty for me." She rummaged around her disorganised desk and passed me over a ten by eight black and white photograph.
"Here he is. Thinking more your type?"
I looked at the photo and my stomach plummeted. It was Xavier

with his arm around a beautiful blonde socialite leaving a club in London. Holy. Shit. What was he doing back in London? No. This wasn't happening. I couldn't do it. Even if my creative writer juices were flowing at the thought…it was impossible for me and him to ever meet again. *Ever.*

Harriet observed me intently, her journalist instinct and eyes very much on alert. "So, *he* is your type…"

I took a deep breath and nonchalantly slid the photo back across the desk to her. "Sorry Harriet. I must pass on this one."

Harriet watched me for a long moment. "You won't reconsider?"

I stood up my stomach churning and my legs weak. I shook my head. "Afraid not."

I had almost got to the door before she added "Not even if he says he won't do the interview with anyone else but you…?"

I twirled around. "What?"

"When our magazine approached him, he phoned me personally to ask for you and you alone."

"Why would he do that?" the question was meant more for me than Harriet, but she answered anyway.

"Says that he thinks he met you once in Paris…did he?"

I took a deep breath. It would be useless to try and lie to Harriet. She was too good at fathoming out liars from twenty feet away. "Yes. We did. Briefly."

"What happened?"

Everything…

"Nothing. We met in a café. He bought me a coffee and invited me to dinner. I declined. Perhaps he is still annoyed? Who knows? I doubt I made that much of an impression on him…I surprised he remembered me…"

I remember him though…every single beautiful, delicious inch of him….

"He remembered enough about you to describe you to me in infinite detail, but he says he never got your number or your surname."

I looked at her suddenly alarmed. "You didn't give him my number?"

She sat back in her chair and rolled her eyes. "Not that stupid Alyssa. But he knows you freelance here. Is that going to be a problem?"

After Paris

Fuck. Yes.
"No, of course not. Why would it be?"
"You tell me Alyssa. A hot, red-bloodied handsome eligible man is asking about you and you seem to be running away with your tail between your legs. What really happened in Paris?" Harriet narrowed her eyes and stared at me waiting for my answer.
How about my whole world got turned upside down? How about I have been celibate for six months as no man ever matches up to him? How about I still dream about that night in Paris, and I can't erase it from my memory?
I crossed my fingers behind my back and forced a smile to my lips. "Nothing at all Harri. I still have no idea why he would remember me."
"Hmmm. Well anyway think about it. He wants you and I don't think he is going to take no for an answer."
"There is categorically no way I am going to write the piece on him," I opened the office door and turned back to her. "I hope you get someone else to do it."
"Alyssa...." Harriet's voice was soft making me turn back to her. "I shall let him know."
I nodded and left. *Holy fucking shit.*

After leaving the office I walked along the Embankment as if on auto pilot and tried to clear my head. What the hell? I never expected this is a million years.
That night with him in Paris is so clearly still etched in my mind. His kisses, his hands touching and stroking my skin, his perfectly sculpted body moving in unadulterated synchronisation with mine, his eyes burning down at me, the feeling of absolute satisfaction as I watched him unravel as he fell over the edge and gave me everything. The way he held me afterwards, like we were not two strangers in strange surroundings but like what had just happened between us was meaningful and perhaps, just perhaps, had a future. I watched him as he slept and wished that things were different, wished that I had accepted his offer of dinner and that he knew exactly who I was. I wanted so badly to hear my name on his lips as he reached the peak of carnal pleasure. I felt a connection with him that I had never felt before with any man and it had hurt that I had been just a nameless, faceless stranger

in his bed. When he asked me to remove my mask, I had been so tempted. I wanted him to see it was me, the woman he had met at the café, wanted him to know. But I couldn't and I didn't.

Of course, when I got back to London a few days later, I had put his name in my search engine and hundreds of photos of him had popped up on my screen, mostly with models, actresses and socialites both Parisian and British. He was very much an eligible bachelor and was seemingly desired by women by both sides of the Channel as well as further afield too. His good looks, charm and impeccable pedigree made him a very hot piece of news, in fact I was surprised he had never come to my attention before I had even met him, but somehow, he hadn't. A couple of months after I had returned from Paris, I had stopped looking at the internet stories on him, usually with a different woman on his arm at some gala event or a film premiere or something equally as glamourous. All it did was depress me, made my insides churn and my heart break just a tiny bit more every time I saw his handsome face, smiling at the camera without a care in the world and a beautiful woman always by his side. I thought I was doing well. Thought I could be almost ready to move on and now he was here in London, the same city as me. Shit! And furthermore, he knew where I worked and my name. Shit again!

There was a big black range rover parked outside my small, terraced house in Pimlico when I returned home that evening. My heart sank as I knew who it was before I had even reached it. I asked myself how he had found my address but then I guess a man with his network could find almost anything he wanted to. I contemplated making a hasty retreat but was out of luck because just as I turned heel and was about to run, that chocolatey velvet voice called out behind me.
"Alyssa. Fancy bumping into you here."
I closed my eyes and counted to ten before turning to face him. Oh. My. God. Could this man get any more handsome? He was dressed in a dark navy suit that looked like it had been handmade for him, and it probably had to be fair. The shirt was white and his tie navy polka dot. He looked absolutely delectable especially when he held his head on one side to smile at me and his dark

After Paris

hair flopped into his eyes. He pushed it back with those wonderfully talented fingers of his and I wondered how on earth I was going to gain any sort of immunity towards this man when just one look at his face could reduce me to mush in about ten seconds flat. Silently I berated myself for being so predictable and so fucking weak and then plastered a false smile on my face for the second time that day.

"Don't tell me...you were just passing," I said as normally as I could.

"You don't look surprised to see me," he walked towards me, and my heart began to beat harder in my chest.

"Any salt cellars headed your way lately?" I couldn't help but mention as I neatly sidestepped his observation. My heartbeat gathered speed as a huge grin appeared on his handsome face.

"I seem to have cleaned up my act since we last met. No flying objects aimed at my head in the past six months although I deserved a few I must admit, probably with a bit of pepper added for good measure."

I'll bet. I had lost count of the number of women he had been seen with but to mention that here would mean he would know I have been keeping tabs on him...which I hadn't obviously....

He stopped in front of me and allowed his eyes to roam my face. It wasn't particularly intense, but I could still feel my face begin to heat.

"Why are you here?" I asked as I tore my eyes away from his to stare at the pavement as I regained my composure.

"In London? Or outside your house?"

"Both."

"In London for work and I think you know why I am here outside your house."

I looked at him and he smiled.

Don't smile at me like that otherwise all my resolve will disappear.

"Why won't you write the article about me?" he asked softly.

"I'm still working on my book. I have deadlines..."

"Your boss lady Harriet wants you to do it. She agrees with me that you are the best person for the job, but she says you were adamant that you wouldn't."

"Because I am busy."

"She says that you could do it if you really wanted to."
"Then perhaps I don't really want to."
"It really should be me who is being pissy..."
My eyes snapped to his and I let out a snort. "I beg your pardon?"
"You didn't call me. Not once. You had my number."
"Is this what this is all about? Because I didn't call you?" I shook my head in amazement. He had hardly been pining for me. I had seen photographic proof of that. I went to walk past him, and he reached out and gently grabbed my arm and pulled me round to face him. My heart was beating so fast now I thought he must surely hear.
"Yes, I admit I am a bit pissed you didn't call me, but it is not about that. I want you to write it because you are a good writer, I've read your work and plus we already have a connection. I feel like I know you...is that stupid? I know we only met for what? Half an hour outside a café in Paris but I just feel comfortable with you. Please think about it at least?"
I closed my eyes for a second. I needed to move away from him. He smelled divine, just like I remembered, and it was bringing everything about Paris back to me. If I could bottle that smell and sell it, I would make a fortune. I pulled my arm away and he let me go.
"I need to sleep on it. I'll let Harriet know tomorrow," I began to walk away.
"I can't believe that you are not going to even invite me in for a coffee..." his voice held a laugh.
"Believe it," I called over my shoulder without turning as I strode the short distance to my house with so much more confidence than I felt.
I closed my front door behind me and stood there trying to control my nerves and my shaking hands. Then I ran upstairs and watched him from my bedroom window as he stood on the pavement looking at my house for a while. He was smiling and shaking his head. Probably couldn't believe that a woman had turned him down not once but twice. Then he climbed into his car and sat there for a few minutes more until at last he started the engine and drove away.

After Paris

I slumped against the wall in my bedroom and slowly slid down to the floor into a seated position and hugged my knees to my chest. I already knew I was going to do it. How could I not? But this was dangerous territory. I needed to detach myself from him and yet at the same time get to know him enough to draw the story out and to find out all I could. I leant my head back against the wall and closed my eyes. Now, how the hell was I going to do that?

CHAPTER FIVE

Xavier

I thought I was beyond being surprised. I thought there was not anyone or anything out there that could surprise me and yet she had. Alyssa James. When the magazine had approached me, my first reaction was to decline but then I saw that the Alyssa I had met in Paris was the same Alyssa James that now worked freelance for *Aristocrat* magazine. I had done my research after that meeting in the café and looked her up on the internet straight away and there she was. She looked like a model, but much more beautiful and her résumé read like a literary who's who. Her articles were well written and honest, and she always brought something new to the table. She was smart and beautiful, which was a lethal combination in my books, and I wanted her, both in the professional sense and the personal sense. But it was obvious that she wasn't interested. She hadn't called and I was not into chasing women…. until now.

For some reason ever since meeting Alyssa in Paris I hadn't been unable to get her out of my mind. It was strange but I had met her on the same day that I went to Masquerade…the same day I had met the other woman I couldn't seem to erase from my memory…the one that had seriously blown my mind. I had done some investigating there too. The owner of the club of course would tell me nothing, even after I asked Eduardo to intervene

After Paris

on my behalf. The only information he came back with was what I already knew. She was there for one night only. They didn't even have her real name. She had disappeared off the face of the earth. I dreamt of her sometimes but even in my dreams she wore a mask, and I could never see her face. I always woke up with a massive hard on that hurt like hell and so I often had to relieve myself in the shower like some adolescent sixteen-year-old boy. That was another thing, ever since that night in Masquerade I had almost hated having sex. Somehow every woman I met could not live up to my expectations of that memorable night with *Papillon*, as I had named her. I let them take me in their mouth just to relieve my pent-up frustration and then fucked them hard and fast but after that I just wanted them gone. I knew I was being a selfish, arrogant, bastard but there was nothing I could do about it, and I began to wonder if I would ever be sexually satisfied again. But now Alyssa was back in my life, and I thought that maybe, just maybe, the pleasure would return. However, going by our meeting today I didn't hold out much hope. Alyssa seemed indifferent to me and that was something I was not used to. Women either loved me or hated me and to be honest they usually hated me because they really loved me. Alyssa James was an enigma. Her body language was cold and detached but her eyes seemed to burn into my soul. I saw the subtle flush of her skin when I looked at her for a moment too long, noted how she tried to keep her eyes from mine, felt the tremor of the body when I touched her arm. I knew it wasn't going to be easy getting Alyssa into my bed but something about that made me relish the challenge. It had been ages since a woman resisted me the way she did, on all levels, but I was ready to break them down one by one and the first one was getting her to write the article about me.

I sat down with a thump on my sofa and after undoing the laces, toed off my shoes. I pulled at my tie and let it hang around my neck like a noose. Alyssa James had me just like this tie. I sat back and rested my head on the back of the sofa, closed my eyes and stretched my legs out. My phone buzzed. I opened one eye to see who was calling me. It was Eduardo. I slid my phone to answer and breathed a long sigh. "Ed, what's up?"

"What's up with you mate? Thought you were meeting me and Gabe for drinks tonight?"

I looked at my watch. It was 7pm already. Could I be bothered to get ready and meet the boys? All I wanted to do was to have a shower and watch something mind numbing on the television.

"Not feeling it Ed. I am just going to have a shower and veg out here on the sofa. Maybe order some Indian food and chill."

"We'll be there in half an hour," Ed said laughing. "Don't bother saying no, Gabe is already ordering an Uber as we speak. Just make sure you order enough food for us. We'll bring the booze."

I laughed even though I really did want to just chill out on my own this evening. Maybe some company would get me out of this mood. "Yeah ok. See you soon."

I headed for the shower, dialing the rather splendid Indian restaurant near to me as I walked. I ordered enough food for all of us and then stripped off and gratefully slid under the hot cascading water. I had just stepped out ten minutes later when I heard the doorbell. Couldn't be the Indian as they said they would need forty minutes to prepare the food. Perhaps Gabe and Ed had been nearer than they'd thought. I wrapped a fluffy white towel around my waist and padded through the lounge to the hallway. I looked through the spy hole. Alyssa? *What the fuck?*

I was so surprised to see her there that I threw open the door without thinking and then realised my state of dress or undress and I decided to blag it.

"Miss James…"

Her eyes wandered over my body, and I couldn't help but stand a bit straighter as I subconsciously pushed my shoulders back and my chest out. I worked out a lot and my body had never been in better shape. And it helped that a recent jaunt to the south of France had my skin tanned and smooth. I was totally more than ok with her checking me out, which she was doing quite surreptitiously, pretending to look anywhere else but at me. Her cheeks coloured a beautiful shade of pink….so not totally immune to me then? Interesting…

"To what do I owe this pleasure?"

"Sorry, I should have called," She pushed her hair back and tucked a tendril behind her ear as she stared down at the ground.

After Paris

"It is obviously inconvenient for you."
She went to walk away, and I found myself in some sort of mild panic.
"It's not inconvenient, please come in...have a drink..."
She looked back and smiled. "At least you have more manners than me. I am sorry I was rude earlier. You just took me by surprise...turning up at my house like that."
"So, you thought you would pay me back?" I grinned.
She shook her head and rolled her delectable lips together to stop a smile forming. "No. I was just in your area; meeting some friends for drinks and thought I would drop by and tell you that I will do it...the story on you. You were right. I have made time in my diary, and we can begin whenever you are ready."
I smiled at that news. I was looking forward to working with her already...seeing her every day.
"Come in. Please. At least have a drink. There's some Indian food being delivered in a moment if you're hungry?"
She shook her head. "No, really. I have intruded on your time enough as it is." She backed down the steps that led to my front door. "Just call Harriet when want me to start."
I watched as she walked away.
"What did you mean?" I called as she reached the pavement. "When you said that I was right?"
She turned and smiled. "About the connection between us..."
She raised her eyebrows and nodded her head as a greeting for goodbye and disappeared down the street. I almost ran after her but then remembered again that I was dressed in a towel. Fuck! I smacked the door frame with the palm of my hand. I should have been more insistent that she came in but seeing her standing on my front doorstep had made me nervous. Yes, she made me nervous, and I was never nervous, not ever. Not when I was standing in front of an audience at a seminar or facing of the whole board of directors or naked in front of a new woman and yet here I was with my heart hammering in my chest like some schoolboy on his first date.

"So, you found her then?" Eduardo asked as he put the last piece of naan bread in his mouth. "Thank fuck for that. Maybe it will

37

stop you moping around."
I snorted. "I haven't been moping."
Gabe Elliott, my other best friend, laughed and sipped his beer. "Please. You have been like a bear with a sore head these last few months. What's so special about this woman anyway?"
Everything...
"Look I just like her that's all. She's intelligent and beautiful and she is resisting me at every turn," I grinned.
No need for either of them to know my true feelings towards Alyssa...true feelings? What true feelings?
"Immune to the Montgomery charm huh?" Gabe laughed. "Unbelievable. I need to meet this woman and shake her hand."
I sighed and shook my head. "You two will never understand. Such philistines. I do actually have a heart you know. It's not always about sex."
Eduardo laughed out loud, and Gabe joined in. Sometimes I wondered why I considered them my friends.
"Holy shit," Eduardo laughed. "I have heard it all now."
"So, you don't want to fuck her then? Is that what you're saying?" Gabe swigged back some more beer and shook his head in amazement.
I grinned. "Of course, I do...but I have decided that I am going to hold back. This woman is different. I need to take my time. I need to woo her."
"She will hear the background of your family and run a mile anyway," Eduardo grinned. "Does your mother know you are doing this story?"
"No. She is living a very calm and stress-free life in Monaco and doesn't need to know. The less my mother gets involved in my affairs the better it is."
Gabe leant forward and raised his eyebrows. "Is this story going to be a no holds barred exposé? Are you going to tell the irresistible Alyssa your deepest darkest secrets?"
I let out a short sharp laugh. "I don't know. I suppose the journalist in her will want to uncover my colourful and illustrious past in some way. I mean it is hard to ignore, isn't it? But I am hoping it will be more about me here and now, and what I am trying to achieve in the new company."

After Paris

"Well, you are the youngest CEO of a FTSE company at the time of writing, plus you are a playboy of category A status, and you have an actress for a mother. Even I can't wait to read it," Eduardo grinned. He wriggled his eyebrows. "And you have the hots for the journalist writing it…should be interesting…"

I sat back and swirled my whisky around my glass and contemplated. How would Alyssa feel once all my skeletons had come out of the proverbial closet? The press had already torn us a family to shreds in the past but none of them had ever uncovered the truth, not the real truth, so far, they had only speculated. My father had a lot to answer for and what was that saying? The sins of the father…

I forced a smile to lips. "Any more drinks gentlemen?"

Alyssa

I stared at my computer screen and all I could see were broad shoulders, a flat stomach, abs-to-die-for and lots and lots of smooth tanned skin, smooth apart from the smattering of chest hair across that hard wall of muscle that trailed down in a tantalisingly thin line to below where his towel gripped low on his waist and clung to his slim hips. I closed my eyes and tried hard to erase the image from my mind. Nope - not working. I had forgotten what a perfect specimen of a man Xavier Montgomery was and when he had opened the door looking like he did, it had momentarily blown my mind. I found myself numb with embarrassment and forcing myself not to look at such masculine perfection was much harder to do than I had ever thought possible especially when I knew what that body was capable of eliciting in me…. things that no one else had ever managed to make me feel. I sighed loudly. Now I had to work with him every day for at least a week or two. The path of temptation was leading right to my door. Oh hell. I shook my head and sighed again. Why was I torturing myself? I mean there was no way I was going there again, not that I had as myself of course, but as a masked stranger I had gone there and then some.

To this day I still did not know what possessed me to approach Xavier in that club and do all the things we did that night. I could feel my cheeks burning now just thinking about what we did, the way he made me feel, the total abandonment of any kind of sense as his hands touched me, stroked me, caressed me. I had never felt that way before with my body trembling and tiny bursts of pleasure reaching every part of me. I felt as if I had found the other half of me, well sexually anyway. It was as if we were lovers and not just having sex for one night in a sex club in Paris.

And there it was. The truth.

To Xavier Montgomery I was a stranger with whom he had had a hot and steamy encounter within a sex club. I bet he did those kinds of things all the time. To him I was probably just another woman to add to his brief encounters collection. The thought sickened me. I bet he didn't even rate the sex we had had as great sex. Yes, he had moaned like he meant it and whispered dirty words in my ear, but he probably did that to all the women he slept with. I remembered his deep voice telling me over and over how sexy I was, how desirable and when he lapsed into French, oh my God.

But they were just words spoken to a stranger.

I stared at my screen some more and an email pinged onto the screen in the right-hand corner. I saw it was from Harriet. I clicked to open it and read the subject - Xavier Montgomery. My eyes scanned the email and my stomach tied itself into thousands of knots. Mr. Montgomery wanted me to start tomorrow and to be at his offices in Mayfair at 8.30am sharp so that I could sit in on a Board meeting. And so, it begins.

CHAPTER SIX

Alyssa

I looked at my watch. It was 8.00am and I was walking down the street to the Montgomery Capital building. The knots had transformed into butterflies in my stomach and my mouth was dry with nerves. I really had to get over this. I had to be cool, calm, and collected and couldn't let anything get in the way of my professionalism, something I had always prided myself on. I could see the building in front of me; glass fronted, sleek hard lines, the company name written in gold lettering on the doors. There was an understated elegance in that it was almost like one of those fancy designer shops on The Champs Élysées in Paris and just like that, I already had an angle, a caption...*boutique finance*. I was a bit early but sometimes I liked to catch my subject off guard when they least expected me and weren't quite ready. I had decided to make an early call on Xavier Montgomery.

I was signed in by a very attractive blonde on reception and handed a visitor lanyard with my name on it. I was told to go up to the executive floor where Mr. Montgomery would be waiting for me. The butterflies circled some more as the lift went up to the executive floor and when the doors opened holy shit...there was Xavier waiting right outside the lift doors for me. The butterflies took flight. He looked like a million dollars in his dark

grey bespoke suit with a white shirt and grey paisley patterned tie. He also looked edible. His just-got-out-of-bed hair was still a bit damp, I guessed from his morning shower, and it made it seem even darker against the tan of his skin and the blue of his eyes and the fullness of his lips…. *rein it in Alyssa…*
I took a deep breath and smiled my professional megawatt smile.
"Good morning, Mr. Montgomery."
He smiled and raised an eyebrow. "So formal Alyssa? The last time you saw me I was wearing just a towel…"
Absolutely no need to remind me.
My eyes darted around nervously wondering if anyone else had heard that. He laughed softly.
"Don't worry, no one here yet, just you and me for the moment. My assistant gets here at 8.30am. Would you like a coffee? I just made a fresh pot."
I let out a breath that I wasn't aware of holding and smiled.
"I would love a coffee." I can't believe he had made his own coffee.
He watched me for a moment and then said "In that case follow me…"
I looked around at the furnishings and luxury surrounding me as I followed him. It was glass everywhere, with marble floors and gold touches in the artwork and pieces of sculpture and then another thought hit me. *Midas Montgomery. Everything he touches turns to gold…* and just like that I had the by line of my interview. His office did not disappoint either. What did I expect? There were huge cream comfy sofas in one corner, a magnificent antique desk in the centre and the smell of freshly brewed coffee.
"Have a seat," he smiled as he went over to the coffee machine. "How do you like it?"
"Like what?" I stammered as I sank into the plush soft cushioned seating of the sofa.
He looked at me for a long second before raising both eyebrows this time. "Your coffee?"
"Oh yes of course…em…white, one sugar please."
I looked around some more as Xavier poured the coffee. There were some photos on his desk that I couldn't see, and I longed to get up and go and see who they were of maybe some rich,

After Paris

beautiful fiancée? And why did that thought fill me with disappointment? He walked toward me with two white porcelain cups and saucers in his hands and placed one on front of me on the elegant antique coffee table and then sat down opposite me with his own coffee in his hand. He took a sip whilst watching me as I fiddled nervously in my bag getting my notepad and pen out ready. I was old school, preferring to write down my observations as well as using taped material.

"Starting work already Alyssa?" he asked undoing his jacket buttons with one hand and sitting back. "Why don't you just relax and drink your coffee first?"

"I just like to be prepared," I answered meeting his eyes for the first time since he had sat down.

"Were you a girl guide by any chance?" he grinned and then let out a short sharp breath as he caught my non-amused glare. "Sorry, bad joke."

I sipped my coffee staring at him. "Bad joke, but the coffee is good at least. You have something redeemable."

"Wow! That's a bit of a harsh judgement to make, you hardly know me yet," He smiled but it didn't quite reach his eyes and I knew I had hit a nerve.

"At the end of our time together I am going to know more about you than you know yourself," I smiled feeling the ball was in my court for the first time since I had met him. "And my first impressions are not good."

He sipped his coffee calmly and then raised his eyes to mine. "And what are your first impressions?"

"A rich, privileged, spoilt, womaniser with a brilliant mind for making money for himself and his equally rich clients. A ruthless businessman who hides behind his charm and boyish behaviour along with his childhood friends, Gabe Elliott and Eduardo Espinosa who are also equally as rich, spoilt, and privileged as he is."

He put his cup down calmly and his eyes when they met mine were like a stormy sea. Good he is rattled. "Is that all you have Miss James?"

"No. I have a lot more…unfortunately it is more of the same. I hope that is not all I am going to find though."

"So sorry that my past life is not impressive enough for you," He interrupted, his voice calm and in control even though his blue eyes blazed into mine.

I wasn't fazed. I had the reaction I wanted and so I sat back and crossed my legs in my knee length skirt. My legs were still slightly tanned from my holiday in Santorini. He wasn't the only one who could flaunt a tan. I watched as his eyes diverted to my legs and bit my lip to stop my smile. *Game on...*

"Let's hope there is more to you than meets the eye Mr. Montgomery, otherwise my story is going to be so clichéd and boring. I am a good writer, but not even I can pretty up what I have found so far."

He stared at me and did that thing that made me melt, he stared at my mouth and then slowly met my eyes again.

"Then we had better hope you are as good as you say you are."

I smiled and took out my writing pad and pen and wrote something on the first page and then closed it again.

"What did you write?" he asked pretending not to be in the slightest bit bothered.

"Predictable."

He laughed and stood up and then walked over to me and stood with his legs each side of mine. He bent down and rested his hands on the back of the sofa caging me in so that his delectably handsome face was only inches from my own.

"You will learn a lot of things about me Miss James, and one of the things you will learn is that I am never predictable..." His full lips were tantalisingly close to mine and for one wild moment I actually thought he was going to kiss me and God, I actually wanted him to.

A knock on the door broke the tense moment and Xavier stood up looking towards the door.

"Come in," he called. Was it my imagination or had his voice deepened just a tad?

A tall red head poked her head around the door.

"Good morning, Mr. Montgomery," she smiled and then smiled at me.

Xavier walked back to his desk running a hand through his hair.

"Morning Estelle. Come in and meet Alyssa James. She is going

After Paris

to be shadowing me for the next week or so. Please make sure that she is booked in on all my meetings both during working hours and after working hours too please."

Estelle walked towards me, and I stood up straightening my skirt as I did so. I held out my hand.

"It's lovely to meet you, Estelle."

"Lovely to meet you too Miss James."

"Call me Alyssa please."

She nodded and smiled. "Alyssa. I shall make sure that you are everywhere Mr. Montgomery is for the next week."

I laughed. "Oooh…no need to go that far. I am sure Mr. Montgomery will be sick of seeing my face soon."

I glanced over at him, and he raised his eyebrow but remained silent.

"The board members are arriving Mr. Montgomery," Estelle said to him. "Everything has been set up. I have laid out refreshments and everything you need. I have put Miss James, sorry Alyssa, next to you. Is that ok?"

Xavier refastened his jacket and pushed his hair back with his fingers. "That is great Estelle. Thanks."

Estelle gave me a bright smile before she left, closing the door behind her.

I opened my pad and wrote something and then closed it again. He frowned. "Really?"

"What?" I feigned innocence.

"One word each time?"

"I wrote more than one word that time."

"Thank God, because if you are writing one word at a time you and I are going to be in each other's company for a lot longer than a week."

"God forbid," I muttered with a false smile.

He smirked. "What did you write this time? Looks good in a suit?"

I snorted a laugh. "None of your business…my notes are my own. I wanted to ask you, do you mind if I record the interview with you, obviously not in the boardroom because that would be confidential, but on other occasions?"

He frowned again. "Like when?"

"When it is just you and I talking."
He shrugged. "Yes. Fine. I can't see a problem. Now let's go to this board meeting."

Xavier

Fuck me. I couldn't concentrate. The board meeting was dragging on and all I wanted to do was to take Miss Uptight-in-a short-skirt out to lunch and grill her about what she knew and why she felt such animosity towards me. It annoyed me beyond belief that she thought so little of me and had me down as a spoilt little rich boy, which technically I was of course, but that was not *all* I was. For some insane reason I wanted her to like me, I wanted her to see me for who I was now, who I had become. Sure, my much-publicised antics hadn't helped me at all, and in fact there were quite a few sitting around this board table now that would agree with Alyssa and seriously like to give me a good dressing down. Some of them had tried to take me aside in the past admitting that they would like to see me on the financial pages of the nationals more and the gossip columns less. Somehow it always seemed that when I was out having fun, there was a reporter ready to take some stupid photo of me leaving a restaurant or club with some woman in tow.

I glanced sideways to look at her and she was scribbling away in that notebook of hers as she listened to Mark Winters, Head of IT, drone on about a new software programme that he thought would be good for the company. Mark was good at his job, but IT was not on my list of interests. That is what I paid him for. To make sure we had the best software going and not to go into technical IT language that none of us around this table, apart from him, could understand. I held up my hand to stop him. He paused and looked at me.

"Let me ask you something Mark…"

"Of course, Xavier. Go ahead."

"Do you think that this is a software programme we need?"

He nodded. "Without a doubt it's the best out there because…"

I held up my hand again. "Mark. Just buy it ok?"

After Paris

The whole room was silent looking at me.
Mark cleared his throat and looked at me for a long moment unsure of what he had just heard me say. "Just like that?"
I raised my eyebrows. "Yep. Just buy it."
"You are sure? You know it costs…"
I looked down at my paperwork in front of me and the neat spreadsheet of figures Mark had prepared. "…A million pounds to install? Yep."
"And running costs," he faltered not quite sure why it had been so easy to get me to sign along the dotted line.
"Another million at least?" I jumped in. "That's fine. If it as good as you say it is then we shall reap the rewards in what six months?"
"To a year," Mark added. "On the outside."
"Great. We can recoup that money back in no time. Get the papers sent up to me and I will sign it off."
Mark beamed. "Ok. I will do. Great. Thanks."
I smiled and looked at the agenda. "Any more business?"
I looked around the table almost daring one of them to say something. Thank God they all remained silent.
"No? Good. Have a good day ladies and gentlemen and I shall see you in two weeks."
I watched as the board members filed out of the room and then turned to Alyssa who was watching me carefully.
"What?" I asked leaning back in my chair.
"Two million just like that?"
I laughed. "Yes."
"That poor man thought he was going in for the hard sell…"
"And so, I made it easy for him."
"Why?"
"Because I am getting hungry, and I want take you to a special restaurant that I know for lunch."
She looked at her watch. "Xavier, it's 10.30 in the morning."
"Yes, and it takes a couple of hours to get where I want to go and so we have to leave now."
She sat back and stared at me incredulous. "You know I am working right? This is not just some whirlwind of lunches and dinners and stupid fancy parties. I am here to get to know you

47

and what you do. I am not one of your girlfriends and I don't need to be wined and dined."

"I know. But this is what I do. You want to know the real me? Then come to lunch with me."

She stood up. "Please do not tell me that your life is as shallow as I think it is."

I stood up to face her, my own anger now beginning to bubble to the surface. Why did she keep bringing this up? "My life is not shallow."

She gathered up her things and slung them in her bag.

"Then please do me a favour and save your smooching and your lunching and your 'whatever else you think you are doing' for one of the other gullible airheads you date and don't waste your time trying to get me to go to some fancy restaurant for lunch because you think it will impress me because it won't. I am a serious journalist and if you don't want to treat this story as serious too then we are finished. Right here and now."

Holy fuck. This woman had surely been put on this earth to infuriate me but strangely as much as the fury stirred inside me, lust took over me and all I could think about was that I wanted to bend her over this boardroom table and shimmy that tight little skirt of hers up her thighs and sink myself into her until she begged me to stop. She was sexy as hell when she was mad…like a live wire. Her dark eyes were ablaze with an inner fire. Surely, she must feel it too. This thing between us. Undefinable and yet so tangible that you could almost touch it.

"Well?" she asked in an exasperated voice. "What's it to be?"

I was in front of her in two seconds flat. It was like I was a vampire in one of those movies where they move at lighting speed. I grabbed her face in my hands and crushed my lips onto hers. She tasted of coffee and a hint of mint, and her lips were soft and yielding as against all the odds she kissed me back. Her bag dropped to the floor with a loud thud but neither of us cared as the kiss became deeper, all consuming, as her mouth opened slightly more, and my tongue delved inside capturing hers. I heard her moan against my mouth, a small feminine moan that had my insides turn to mush and my cock harden inside my trousers. I pressed myself against her and she moaned again. I

After Paris

had never wanted to fuck a woman so much in my life…well maybe just that woman in Paris that night, my masked *Papillon*. I was relentless with the kiss and the deeper it got the more I wanted her. My hands tangled in her hair at the nape of her neck as I pulled her closer. My body seemed to have a will of its own as it pushed against hers and bloody hell, she felt good. All soft curves behind that very professional morally upright suit of hers. She smelled divine…like…like…

Suddenly she broke away pushing me against my chest with both hands. We stared at each other breathless for about a nano second before she spoke.

"What the fuck was that?" she breathed, her eyes were still dark with desire, but they were now also full of anger and incomprehension.

I ran a nervous hand through my hair and thought I would go for the romantic approach. "An unbelievable kiss?"

"What is it you are not getting?" she asked bending to pick up her bag. "Are you out of your tiny mind? What have I just told you? I am not one of your women. I am here to work," she pointed an accusing finger at me. "And you Mr. Montgomery have overstepped the line."

I sat on the boardroom table and crossed my feet at the ankles and my arms over my chest. "Fine Alyssa. Just keep ignoring the signs, this thing between us."

She threw both of her arms in in the air. "What thing? For fuck's sake. Do you honestly think that every woman you meet is just going to fall hopelessly at your feet?"

I pondered that one with a smile and I saw her scowl.

"Unbelievable," she gasped, shaking her head.

"So what? We are just going to ignore that kiss?" I asked. Is she for real? That kiss was mind blowing, absolutely sublime. Shit, my cock was still hard from that kiss. I could only imagine that sex with her would be amazing.

"Yes, we are going to ignore that kiss. It should never have happened and if it happens again, I am off the story. I mean it." Alyssa glared at me like she really did mean it. Fine. I loved a challenge and she had just thrown down the gauntlet. She stormed over to the door and threw it open.

Jacqueline Bacci

"Now are you actually going to do some work because I would like to, if that is not too much trouble for you?"
I stood up and walked towards her.
"Is that a 'no' to lunch then?"
She shook her head in disgust and strode angrily into the corridor. I could not help the grin that crept upon my lips as I followed her.

CHAPTER SEVEN

Xavier

We ordered sandwiches from the local deli and ate them in my office. Not exactly what I had in mind but hell I had got some work done that morning. Things I had been putting off for ages. Frosty Knickers had galvanised me into action. She had hardly spoken to me after 'the kiss' and had just observed me working from her little makeshift desk that I had set up for her.
"What are you doing this evening?" she asked as she took a bite of her chargrilled chicken sandwich.
"Nothing. A quiet night in. Thought we could share a supper and you could ask me some of those deep, meaningful questions that you have been saving up. Does that suit you?" I drank some of my water from my glass and watched her over the rim.
She shrugged. "Yes sure. That sounds good. Can I ask you a question now?"
"Fire away,"
"Is anything off limits?"
Only you apparently....
"What do you mean? As in the questions you ask me?"
She nodded.
"No. You can ask me anything you like. I have nothing to hide."
Only all the shit that I am never telling anyone…
I raised my eyes to hers and she was studying me, her head to

one side.

"Everyone has something to hide Xavier," she said softly.

"Do you?"

"Of course."

"Like what?" I sat back in my chair suddenly very interested to know what this beauty before me was hiding.

She put her sandwich down on her plate and took a sip of her diet cola. "Things that I would never tell anyone."

Strange how her words had echoed my thoughts. "You have me intrigued now Miss James."

"Good," She smiled not about to give anything away.

"Do you have a boyfriend?" I asked steeling myself against a positive answer.

She shook her head. "No one special."

"But you are dating?"

She lifted her slim shoulders in a shrug. "Not really...not dating as such..."

I contemplated that answer. So, what was she doing then? One-night stands? Fucking them and moving on? The thought was nauseating. I was so double standards. It was alright for me to do but the thought of Alyssa doing the same turned my stomach.

"What then? You don't seem the type to fuck around."

She raised her eyebrows at that but remained silent.

"So, you do have one-night stands?" *Fuck. I was getting pissed off.*

"Really none of your business," she answered calmly. "And how did we get onto this subject anyway?"

She pulled her notebook towards her and wrote something and then closed it before I could see. "Before you ask me, I wrote two words. Hypocritical Bastard. Happy?"

I laughed. "Not true but funny."

This woman was good at reading between the lines. She thought I was angry because I didn't agree with a woman having one-night stands...she was partly right but I was only angry because I didn't agree with *her* having one-night stands. Other women could do whatever the fuck they wanted to.

"So basically, it is ok for you to conduct your life along those lines but not for me to?" She challenged.

Yes, that is so fucking right!

After Paris

"Not what I was saying..." I began before she interrupted my half lie.

"I saw the look of disapproval on your face. I hate to break this to you, but it is the twenty first century. Women can do what they want to with whom they want to whenever they want to!"

"I totally agree..."

"No, you don't," She countered. "Not really."

Not where you're concerned. No, I don't.

"Do you have a girlfriend?"

I snorted a laugh. "Me? Why would I deprive other women of my company to focus on only one? That doesn't make any sense. That's not how to play the game."

She shook her head in disgust. God, it was so easy to wind her up. Enjoyable in fact, and I felt a sliver of satisfaction at being able to annoy her to the extent that I could see her deep dark brown eyes become almost black with anger.

"I don't think I have ever met such a more self-absorbed, arrogant, misogynistic..."

I held up my hand. I really was enjoying this now. "Not misogynistic. I love women. So, you can't call me that."

"What should I call you then Casanova?"

Casanova.... of all the things she could have said she chose that. Suddenly memories of that night in Paris came flooding back to me and I felt an unexpected lurch in my stomach.

Disappointment and anger bubbled up to the surface again and for some inexplicable reason I wanted to take it out on her.

"Call me whatever you want but just not spoilt, rich and privileged because you don't even know me, the real me that is. You only know what the press writes about me. I thought you were better than that Miss James, that you had undertaken serious research. It is beneath you to believe the shit that is written in the gutter press."

She watched me for a long moment, her cheeks tinged with pink from anger, anger directed at me for questioning her abilities as a journalist and writer. She looked beautiful and so very desirable that I wanted to sweep her up in my arms, tear off that tight skirt and fuck her until she begged me to stop.

"You don't do yourself any favours Xavier. All my initial research has only unearthed you pictured with a different woman every time you step outside the door, your reputation for being a playboy, living a very glamourous life in the fast lane and for being ruthless in business. What else do you have to show me? Because I really hope it is more than that?" Her voice was quiet, but clear and precise.

"And I hope you have more than one-word descriptions to offer. I hope your interview is not going to be a mirror of all those that have gone before. I hope you are not going to disappoint me...."

"No, I hope *you* don't disappoint me," she replied, tilting her chin up triumphantly.

I snorted a laugh of derision. "I never disappoint Miss James. You don't need to worry about that."

I was being petty and crass but the meaning behind my words was not lost on her. She glared at me, and I smirked back.

"I do believe that was a feeble attempt at some sort of double entendre Mr. Montgomery and here I was thinking that you were trying to convince me you were more than just a womanising playboy."

God! She was infuriating.

"I was just trying to lighten the mood. Joking aside, I will prove to you that I am nothing of the sort. I may have been once, but that clichéd description no longer applies to me."

"Then let's hope I get more than a glimpse at the man behind the cliché then."

"Why the fuck are we arguing?" I asked throwing the rest of my sandwich onto my plate. I had kind of lost my appetite. "Do you intend to antagonise me at every step of the way?"

She stared at me for a long moment, and I had a feeling that she was mentally counting to ten.

"I must apologise. I wasn't trying to annoy you but if I was, I will consider that a bonus. Plus, we were not arguing we were having a heated discussion."

And just like that this woman had me stumped again and she had just taken the wind out of my sails, and I was for once totally at a loss of what else to say.

She faked a smile and then carried on eating her sandwich, which infuriated me even more. I had never had such diverse feelings

After Paris

towards a woman in my whole life and something told me that this was how it was going to be, her calling me out on my bullshit and me loving every single moment of it.

Alyssa

His house was just as I imagined it would be, sleek lines, minimalist, expensive. All the furniture was expertly placed, and everything had its place. His sofas were huge and comfortable and made of buttery soft caramel leather that I almost melted into as I sat down at his request whilst he fixed me a drink. I watched him as he removed his jacket and tie and flung them onto the other end of the sofa. My heartbeat increased somewhat as he unbuttoned his shirt, and I caught a tantalising glimpse of his neck and hard lean chest.

"Make yourself comfortable," he called over his shoulder as he padded barefoot into the kitchen. Even his feet were perfect, tanned, slim, well groomed. I slipped off my shoes and let my toes experience the soft, fluffy off-white rug that was positioned in front of the sofas and sat back to look around in more detail. My whole house could probably fit into this lounge with room to spare. It was an exquisite room and Xavier obviously has exquisite taste. I could live here forever and never want to leave. Xavier came back with a bottle of champagne and two slim flute glasses.

"Champagne ok for you?" he asked as he began tearing off the foil covering at the top of the bottle.

"Is there a celebration?" I asked raising an eyebrow.

"Alyssa, there doesn't always have to be a celebration to drink champagne. Sometimes you should drink a bottle just for the hell of it," he grinned as the cork popped making me jump slightly. I watched as he poured the sparkling liquid expertly into the flutes and then handed me one "Besides I am celebrating."

I let the bubbles fizz up my nose before asking. "What are you celebrating exactly?"

"That I get to see you every day for the next week or so," he grinned and sat down next to me on the sofa holding out his glass towards mine. "Shall we toast my small nugget of good fortune?" I loved the way he had overlooked our discussion earlier and moved on, liking that the rapport between us had returned to the subtle flirty banter from him and my not-so-subtle rebuffs, which made his blue eyes twinkle, just like they were doing now. Those eyes, as well as the rest of him, were lethal.

I eyed him suspiciously over the rim of my glass. "Are you being sarcastic?"

He frowned. "Not at all…am I sensing that you do not feel as ecstatic as me about us living in each other's pockets?"

"Ok, now you are being sarcastic."

"Fuck, Alyssa. Are you going to toast with me or not?"

I glared at him and reluctantly clinked my glass against his. "Why do I just feel like I have just done a deal with the devil?"

He laughed. "I like that. Hopefully over the next couple of weeks you will allow me to show you that you have not in fact got into bed with the devil, but just a normal, hardworking, fair, totally irresistible guy."

"I don't like your analogy because there will be no 'getting into bed' with anyone, not even figuratively speaking," I took a sip of my champers, and it was delicious. I took another sip. So, not only good taste in furniture but also champagne. What did I expect from a half French playboy? "And by the way, you are not *totally* irresistible."

He so was…totally…

He laughed again and I hated the way my stomach flipped just a little at that rich deep sound. He looked down at my feet.

"What? Is that your idea of getting comfortable? Taking your shoes off?"

"What did you expect? A full striptease?"

His smiling eyes darkened just a tad. "Now there's an idea."

I laughed nervously and reached down to my bag and got my notebook, pen, and mobile phone out of my bag to defuse this conversation.

"Time for work Mr. Montgomery," I smiled fiddling with my phone so that he wouldn't see the way his words had somehow managed to affect me. My mind flitted back to a night in Paris,

After Paris

the way he had stripped the clothes off me, of his naked lean hard body up against mine, the way his lips trailed across my skin leaving a path of goose bumps in their wake. The way he had looked at me as he had moved so skillfully inside me.

Shit...stop it...this is not helping...

Somehow, I managed to find voice record on my phone and placed it on pause between us.

"Ready?" I asked much too brightly, my voice on some higher octave.

He smiled, those lethal blues staring into mine. "Ready when you are."

I asked him everything and he answered everything. He told me about his kind of idyllic childhood growing up in the South of France, mainly with his mother the renowned actress Mirabelle Colbert. His father was Nicholas Montgomery, a diplomat from an aristocratic family who could trace their family tree back to the court of King Henry the Eighth. Their family country estate was in Hampshire, which Xavier informed me he hardly visited. It was well known that his father had divorced his mother about twenty years ago, with the thirteen-year-old Xavier shunted off to France with his mother. He hadn't seen his father much since and it was obvious from his closed and clipped answers on this subject that this had affected him much more than he was ready or willing to admit to me here and now. I knew he was holding back but decided to leave it for now and approach it a bit further down the line when we had established a deeper trust. It wasn't always easy to revisit your past.

Something I could indeed testify to myself.

When I finally looked at my watch, I noted that two hours had gone by just like that. He had been interesting and entertaining and had me laughing a lot at the way he had a laid-back approach to most things in his life, even quite important big things that most other people would consider to be life changing events. He was nonchalant about his position as CEO of a very successful company and of the work he did daily, even when I quoted all the big financial newspaper articles about him. The guy was refreshingly modest about his achievements and rebuffed any kind of accolade that I could throw at him. He would only accept that he had made some good judgements along the way and that they were successful because he had chosen some excellent personnel that worked hard and believed in the company.

Xavier had been upfront and transparent in his answers, and I knew that some editing was needed but I couldn't wait to get back home and start writing. I turned off my record button and stretched my legs out in front of me.

"Thank you for being so open and honest with me," I smiled and for once it wasn't forced. I had enjoyed my time with him.

"Do you think you have some good stuff to go on?" he asked finishing the last of the champagne.

"Definitely," I said bending down to slip on my shoes, ignoring the dizziness I felt from too much of the bubbly stuff. "I don't think I have everything yet, obviously, but I am already writing the beginning in my head."

I yawned and grabbed my bag, stuffing all my things inside. "Well, it has been a long day for me. I am going to head home and start my write up."

"Really? You're leaving? Thought we were grabbing a bite to eat together."

"Xavier, that sounds really good, but I need to go home, have a lovely relaxing bath and then do some work…plus I have had too much to drink and need to get my head straight."

"You barely had three glasses."

I laughed. "I'm a lightweight, what can I say?"

"You could try saying yes to eating with me," he smiled to show that he was just teasing but the truth was I did keep turning him down and that probably was unheard of for Xavier Montgomery.

"Next time, ok?" I said lightly hooking my bag on my shoulder.

"Maybe then I could find out something about you," he said softly as he leant forward and pushed my hair back from where it had fallen across my forehead and into my eyes. The air crackled between us, and I found myself tearing my eyes reluctantly from his and staring at his beautiful feet whilst trying to qualm the fluttering in my stomach and everywhere else in my body.

After Paris

I laughed nervously again. He made me nervous in a good way, a way I wasn't entirely used to.
"That's not exactly how it goes. I interview you remember?" I stood up a bit too quickly and the room whirled around.
He stood up too and looked at me concerned. "Are you ok?"
"I'm fine," I muttered and began walking to the front door. He followed me and I know he was watching me carefully.
"Alyssa," he said getting his mobile out of his pocket. "I'm calling you an Uber."
I waved his suggestion away with my hand. "No need. I can get the tube. I don't live that far away it's only a few stops."
I turned to face him as he tapped his phone totally ignoring me. "The Uber will be in here in five minutes, ok?"
I leant up against the wall near his front door for balance.
"Would you like some water?" he asked.
I shook my head and then immediately regretted it. "No really. I'm fine."
"This is my fault," he said running a frustrated hand through that lovely dark thick hair of his. "I should have given you something to eat with the champagne. You have only had that stupid sandwich today."
"Xavier really. I am absolutely fine."
"Please call me when you get in."
I laughed. "What are you, my mother?"
"Alyssa, please call me."
"I don't know your number."
He got his phone in front of him again. "Tell me yours."
I rattled off my mobile number as he tapped it into his phone.
"I am going to call you and if you don't answer I will come around your house. The Uber is outside waiting."
He opened the door for me and helped me down the steps.
"Xavier! Stop it. I'm not drunk."
He laughed and opened his gate and then the car door. As I climbed in, he repeated about calling him and I just nodded. I needed to get home to bed right now.
He was as good as his word. He called me about a thousand times. The noise of the phone was driving me mad, and I seriously wanted to throw it out of the window. I fumbled about

on the floor by the sofa where I had fallen asleep and found my phone swiping across to answer.

"Hello?"

"For fuck's sake! What the hell Alyssa?" Xavier's booming voice came down the phone. I winced and held it away from my ear.

"I asked you to call me."

"I know, sorry. I had a bath and fell asleep on the sofa."

"Are you ok?"

"Yes, just tired. As you may have guessed I am not a great drinker."

"Yeah, remind me never to take you out with Eduardo and Gabe. You wouldn't last five minutes with those guys."

"I would like to meet them though at some point."

"Yes, and you will…tomorrow night actually."

I winced again as my head throbbed. "What? What do you mean?"

"I have a charity thing to attend. You will need an evening gown as its black tie. It's at The Ritz."

I sighed. "Oh God, I don't think I can keep up with your lifestyle."

He laughed. "Yeah, welcome to my world baby. See you tomorrow at the office. 8.30am sharp."

"Yes of course. See you there."

"Goodnight Alyssa."

My heart jolted at how he said my name, like a caress.

"Goodnight," I whispered.

CHAPTER EIGHT

Xavier

She survived the day. I had to give it to her. She was quiet for once, sitting writing on her laptop and only stopping now and again to ask me some minor questions. She went to see her editor at lunchtime but came back looking refreshed and ready to go again. She joined me on a few meetings and a walk around the different departments. I sent her home early to prepare for the charity ball and now I was outside her house in the limo. I asked the driver to wait and went to knock on her door.
She opened the door and for a moment I was truly speechless. She looked beautiful. Her dress was red, a bright pillar box red and her accessories were all silver. Her hair was hanging in a shiny glossy neat style to her shoulders, and she had red lipstick on...*fuck*. One of my weaknesses was a woman with red lipstick on. There was just something so confident and sexy about a woman who chose that colour on her lips. I stared at her mesmerised until she laughed nervously.
"Well? Do I look ok? I was going to wear another dress but...."
"You look perfect," I said. "Your dress is stunning."
She smiled. "I have a designer friend who has loaned it to me for the night."
"Well, it looks like it was made for you."
She closed her front door and put her keys in her glittery silver bag. I held out my arm and she giggled and linked her arm with mine as I guided her to the car. She smelled divine. Where had I

smelt that scent before?
Now sitting in the car so close to her was driving me crazy. I wanted her so badly, in fact I wanted to tell the driver to take us back home so that I could rip that dress off her and sink myself into her over and over again.

"So, tell me about your friends," she said turning her head towards me.

"Degenerates both of them," I grinned. "Eduardo is a lawyer, Gabe an architect. I have told them to be on their best behaviour around you, but I cannot guarantee it I'm afraid."

"I am sure it will be fine. Do they have girlfriends?"

I rolled my eyes at that one and she laughed.

"I shall take that as a no then."

"Take that as there are not two sane women out there who would want to saddle themselves with those two."

"Have you known each other long?"

"We were all at the same boarding school. We bonded when we found out we all fancied the same girl and then decided that no girl was worth more than our friendship, so we all forgot about the girl and forged our friendship instead."

"Does that happen now? That you all fancy the same woman?"

"Occasionally, but then we all walk away. We have the same principles now as then."

"By the way," she smiled. "Just wanted to say you look very dapper tonight."

I grinned and ran my fingers along the lapel of my bespoke tuxedo. I was strangely chuffed that she noticed and mentioned it.

"So, you do think I am irresistible," I smirked moving a fraction nearer to her.

She sighed and closed her eyes. "Why, oh why, did I have to say anything?" She half whispered under her breath.

I turned to look out of the window, hiding my grin. I loved winding her up.

Walking in the venue I had the strangest urge to take her hand in mine and let everyone there know that she was with me, that she belonged to me. But she didn't of course. Belong to me. Not yet.

After Paris

I watched her smile as her eyes took in all the décor and the decorated tables alight with centerpiece candles in fancy silver candelabras making the beautiful, hired room in the Ritz seem so ethereal. Business associates came to greet me, and Alyssa stood by my side quietly until I introduced her to them and then across the room, I saw Gabe and Eduardo standing by the bar and I touched her arm.

"Come and meet my friends," I said close to her ear. Her hair smelt like lemons and reminded me of the lemon groves we had on our land in the South of France. I inhaled as much as I could without being obvious but when I looked at her, she was looking at me strangely.

"Did you just smell my hair?" she asked with her eyebrows raised in amusement.

"Of course not," I replied momentarily flustered. Was there nothing her journalist eyes missed?

Her sideways look said she was not convinced as she followed me through the crowd of people to the bar.

Gabe, Eduardo and I all greeted each other loudly with slaps on the back and handshaking and then they both turned to look at Alyssa behind me and I pulled her forward.

"Gabe, Ed, I would like you both to meet Alyssa James, the journalist writing the article on me for *Aristocrat* Magazine. Alyssa this is Gabe Elliott and Eduardo Espinosa."

I watched Gabe and Ed's eyes light up and I knew that they both found her attractive. There was no way our 'agreement' was going to come into force with Alyssa. *No fucking way.* I stood back as they greeted her. She shook hands with them.

"Well, I must say this is a pleasure to finally meet you both," she smiled warmly. "I have read and heard so much about you."

"Likewise," Eduardo smiled charmingly, and I threw him a warning look which he completely ignored. "And I must say that you are totally living up to expectations."

She laughed. "Expectations? Wow. What has Xavier been saying about me?"

Gabe grinned. "Let me get you both a drink and we will reveal all."

I sighed and closed my eyes. Holy shit, if this was their best behaviour, I dreaded what they would be like otherwise.

"Just a soft drink for Alyssa," I said before thinking. Both of my friends turned to look at me with an amused wide-eyed look as if to say, 'What the hell dude?'

Alyssa laughed. "It's ok. He's right. I had a bit too much champagne last night and was a bit woozy. A soft drink would be good for now. We can hit the shots later."

Gabe raised a hand to the bartender. "Now that's what I like to hear. Drinks all around."

I looked at Alyssa and she gave me a megawatt smile and I couldn't help but smile back but my gut was twisting with the realisation that the more Gabe and Eduardo drank, the more likely they were to say a bit too much. I had to pull them aside at some point and make sure that didn't happen.

We got our chance during the courses at dinner. We were all sitting on different tables, but I texted them to meet me at the bar when Alyssa went to the ladies' room to powder her nose.

"So, guys," I greeted them whilst calling the bartender over to order some drinks for us all. "What's the verdict?"

"I so would," said Gabe with his hands in his trouser pockets.

"Me too!" grinned Ed. "She's fucking hot."

"Right fuck off both of you and start being serious," I scowled. I knew they were only winding me up, but it actually pissed me off that they were saying it about Alyssa.

They grinned at each other. Ok. So, they had achieved their objective. Ha bloody ha.

I carried on. "Please try to not say anything out of the way. Remember she is a journalist and does not miss a trick. Even if you allude to something she will pick up on it. She already has a very low opinion of the three of us and our messy, much publicised social lives and so please do not add any fuel to the fire." I ordered three Jack Daniels with coke for us and when I looked at my friends, I caught a look pass between them.

"What?" I asked.

"Just how serious are you about her?" Ed grinned.

I snorted a laugh. "What? You know we only have a working relationship."

After Paris

"Soooo," Gabe joined in. "How would you feel if you never saw her again when this interview is over?"
I took a deep gulp of my JD and contemplated. Shit. I hated the thought that I would never see her again. It made my stomach tense up and my chest become tight like I couldn't breathe.
"I guess that would be shit," I owned up. "I like her, and she gives me back as good as I give. She's not intimidated by my wealth, my pathetic celebrity status, or my obvious charm and good looks," I saw them both smirk at that one. "So, I admit I would not be happy if I never saw her again."
"I can see the headlines now. *'Has Xavier Montgomery finally met his match?'*" Gabe laughed.
"Or *'Journalist steals playboy Xavier Montgomery's heart leaving women across the World devastated',*" Ed joined in.
Fuck they were enjoying this. I swigged back the rest of my drink just as I saw Alyssa coming back to our table.
"Did I mention that you two are absolute dickheads?"
I could hear their loud laughter behind me as I made my way back to dinner.

"I like your friends," Alyssa said as I finally held in my arms as we danced.
"I noticed," I replied. "I think you danced twice with Ed and three times with Gabe."
She looked up at me under those long dark lashes of hers. "Oooh, you're counting..."
I laughed. "Yeah anyway, I'm glad you like them. Have they managed to sway you yet?"
"From what exactly?"
"Your preconceived ideas of us and our lives?"
She smiled. "Actually, they have. You didn't tell me that you were the main benefactor of this charity tonight and that you had donated enough to open a new children's wing at the local hospital or that you regularly give some of your time to help with local children's facilities and had all your workforce and your friends help build a new adventure playground all at your own expense."
I winced. "Shit. Those guys talk too much."

"And they are not even drunk," she added wrinkling her nose and pulling a face at me.

"God help us if they were and what they would reveal."

She held her head to one side. "I might stick around and find out some more hidden secrets about you."

"I will tell you all you need to know," I said staring into her eyes. "Eventually."

"Will you?" she asked staring back at me.

"If you come to dinner with me I will."

"Is this because I turned you down in Paris?"

Yes, that had pissed me off, but if she hadn't turned me down then I would never have met the woman in the mask and have had the most satisfyingly sexual experience of my whole life.

I shook my head. "No, of course not. Is that what you think of me? I am not that shallow. I would just like to take you out for dinner. I tend to open up more in a relaxed setting."

"Just as long as it is a working dinner then I suppose I can accept."

I sighed. "Alyssa, why won't you just admit that there is an undeniable attraction between us. Look, it may be because I have had a few drinks tonight, but I am going to come clean. I find you incredibly attractive and sexy and I would like to get to know you better."

"Thought it was the rule that business and pleasure do not mix…"

I snorted a laugh. "Whose rule is that?"

She looked aghast. "Well not yours obviously."

"Do you find me that awful that you can't even contemplate coming to dinner with me? And don't even try and lie to me. When we kissed in the office you were receptive, you were kissing me back and you seemed to be liking it. Correct me if I am wrong here."

"Maybe that's because you are a good kisser and well you are half French so what is a woman supposed to expect? Just because I let you kiss me, and I kissed you back doesn't mean I am going to swoon at your feet. But of course, I don't find you awful. Why would I? Plus, I just found out from your friends that you are like a demi-God or something near that. There are just things about

After Paris

me you don't know. Things that make me the way I am with you."

I was more intrigued than ever. "Which is why dinner would be good, somewhere quiet and intimate where we can talk."

She let out a huge sigh. "Yes, ok, I will come to dinner with you." Taking in my grin of satisfaction, she added "And why do I feel that I have just signed along the dotted line and sold my soul to the Devil again."

I smiled down at her. "I can't be a demi-God and the Devil as well surely?"

She pursed her full red lips. "Hmmm, I am not so sure. If anyone could pull that off it would be you."

I pulled her closer and inhaled her beautiful scent. "So, what side of me do you like best?"

"I'll need some time to find that out…" she smiled sensually.

Fuck, she was so sexy and being so close to her wasn't helping. I pulled away slightly even though that was the exact opposite of what I wanted to do. Just dancing with her was testing all my self-control, add sexy innuendos into the mix and that was just enough to push me over the edge. My trousers had become slightly uncomfortable and the last thing I wanted was for Alyssa to feel my erection. I was like some sixteen-year-old adolescent around this woman.

Gabe and Ed glided past us dancing like a couple in each other's arms, and both Alyssa and I burst out laughing as we watched them acting like complete idiots.

"Are they always like this?" Alyssa laughed.

We, along with the other guests, watched them with amusement as they began to tango around the ballroom.

I shook my head and could not stop grinning. "Absolutely. They are fools."

I couldn't be more grateful to them either. They had diffused a tricky moment and had also been supplying Alyssa with some positive reinforcement of my integrity. God, I loved those guys.

Alyssa

It was getting harder and harder by the minute - resisting him that is. When we were dancing earlier, I nearly melted. I felt boneless. Thank God he was holding me otherwise I would have just melted right into the floor and all that would have been left would have been my red dress in a small steamy heap. Being so close to him was torture.... pure torture. The way he held me, the way our fingers just automatically entwined, the smell of him, how he looked at me, oh just everything. Every. Bloody. Thing. I deserved a medal for the cool act I was putting on. Now he is sitting next to me in the limo taking me home. I love that he hasn't even suggested going to his place which is nearer. He was right. He is definitely not predictable. His phone pinged and he looked at it for a second and then ignored it. He looked at me instead and smiled that melt-your-panties-off smile that he had down to a tee.

"Soooo…. dinner? When shall I book?" He asked as he picked up his phone and tapped something in and then looked at me expectantly.

I was going to fire back something sarcastic and witty but suddenly, the prospect of dinner with him somewhere romantic and secluded seemed suddenly very appealing.

"Whenever it suits you really."

He narrowed his eyes. "What? No story? No excuses? Nothing at all?"

"Nope. When I give my word, I tend to stick to it. Book dinner and I will be there."

He smiled and tapped something in his phone and then swiped it off. "Done. Tomorrow night. It's Friday so not a school night. We can stay out as late as we want to."

I swallowed hard and the nerves racked up a notch, but I plastered a smile on my face. "Great. I shall look forward to it."

He sat back and eyed me suspiciously. "Ok, who are you and what have you done with the spiky journalist who has been at my office lately?"

I giggled. "Listen, I have had a great night, and I am in a good

After Paris

mood. It was fun, your friends are great, and you have been such good company. Also, I have learnt a lot about you tonight which I am going to write down as soon as I get in."

Xavier looked at his watch. "What? It's past midnight. You must be shattered."

"I know but when I have something in my head that I need to write down I need to do it straight away or I lose the momentum. It's the way I work. Sometimes I wake up in the middle of the night with ideas buzzing around in my head and I just need write it all down."

"How's your book coming along by the way?"

"Yeah, it's good. I am in the right place at the moment with it."

"What's it about?"

I looked at him for a long moment. How much shall I divulge at this point? "A bittersweet romance. Set in Paris."

He raised an eyebrow in interest "Which is why you were there? Doing research?"

"*Exactement,*" I replied in my best schoolgirl French.

He slid nearer to me, and I edged over to the door. Then without taking his eyes from mine, he pushed a button, and a screen closed the driver's view of the back seat. *Holy shit! What the hell is he doing?*

"What are you doing?" I asked and couldn't hide the tremor in my voice.

He smiled. "Kissing you."

"I thought we agreed…"

He put his finger to my lips and gently shook his head. "I did not agree to anything."

I put a hand on his chest, a very hard, lean chest, and squirmed into the corner of the car seat.

"Xavier, I don't think this is a good idea."

"Really? I think it's the best idea I've had all night," he put his hand over mine and drew it away from his chest and up to his lips and kissed my palm, whilst keeping his eyes on mine. Oh, my word. Why does he have to be so good at this?

He moved closer and so his face was only inches from mine. His eyes were sparkling as they stared into mine.

"I have been trying so hard to resist you," he whispered. "But I just can't do it to myself anymore."

"I thought the French were so good at resistance," I whispered back.

He smiled. "You always have an answer, don't you?"

I lowered my eyes. "Not always."

He bent his head and kissed my neck very softly. I closed my eyes and let out a tiny moan. I tried, I really tried, not to but it was impossible. His lips on my skin equaled surrender.

"You moan like that, and it just makes me want to kiss you more," Xavier said the words against my skin as he carried on trailing his lips down my neck.

My intention all along was to keep Xavier Montgomery at arms-length but the more he kissed me, the more I felt my resolve deteriorating. But I have too much to tell him before we fall into bed, and I know that we will. The pull, the attraction is too strong. I must tell him about Paris, and I need to tell him about my past. For some reason it is important that I tell him. I want him to know who I am.

One hand is on my thigh, and I can feel the heat through the material of my dress. Oh God. This man is truly irresistible. I want to be naked in his arms, in his bed. I have dreamed about him and that night in Paris for six months and I want it all again but this time I want him to want me and not some masked stranger.

When I opened my eyes, he was looking at me, looking at my mouth and I knew that he was going to kiss me. I wanted him to. I reached out one hand, cradled it around his neck as I forked my fingers in his thick hair curling at the nape and pulled his mouth to mine. He tasted of bourbon and lemons, and I couldn't get enough. His mouth became insistent, forcing my lips apart his tongue found mine. He kissed so perfectly. It was consuming without being too forceful and I was drowning. I reluctantly pulled my lips from his and he moaned.

"Stop resisting Alyssa."

"I have to resist Xavier because if we kiss much more, we are not going to be able to stop and I have things, things I need to tell you."

"Tell me in the morning after I have fucked you all night long…"

After Paris

his words and his eyes were full of lust and want as he lunged for me again.

I shook my head and held one hand against that impossibly hard chest of his. "These things have to be said before we have sex because they may make you feel differently about me."

He leant back and looked at me more seriously now with confusion and a tiny bit of worry in those beautiful Mediterranean blue eyes of his.

"Ok, you are worrying me a bit now Miss James. But just so you know, nothing you tell me will change what I think about you."

I moved my hand from his neck to his cheek and caressed his smooth skin, running my thumb pad over his full lips, slightly swollen from our kiss. "Thank you."

"Can you tell me now?" His eyes dilated slightly and just knowing how he was feeling sent a shiver down my spine and all through my body.

"I will reveal all tomorrow night at dinner."

His mouth curved into an amused smiled and he shook his head. "So... I am on a promise for tomorrow night?"

I smiled coquettishly. "Maybe..."

"You are killing me," he whispered his lips back on mine. He kissed me softly and when we could finally bring ourselves to draw apart, we realised the car had stopped.

Xavier smiled against my lips. "It seems we have arrived at your home."

"I may be a bit late in the office tomorrow morning I need to take my dress back and I have a few errands to run."

He nodded. "Hey look, don't come in tomorrow. We need to leave quite early for dinner so say I pick you up here about 2pm? Is that ok?"

I pulled away from him. "2pm for dinner? That is early."

He smiled. "Trust me, ok?"

I nodded. "Ok."

We got out of the car, and he walked me to my front door and then pulled me against him, held me close and bent his head and kissed my lips again until he drew back reluctantly.

"Until tomorrow then."

"Goodnight Xavier."

"Not happening," he muttered as he walked away. "Endless cold showers for me, so no, I won't have a good night."
I laughed as I waved goodbye, and I was still laughing as I walked up my stairs and went for my own cold shower.

CHAPTER NINE

Alyssa

"Soooo," Naomi Astley beamed at me as I walked through her studio door with my dress the next day. "How was it?"
"I had a great time," I smiled sitting down at her huge table which she used for cutting the material to make her wonderful creations. "The dress was a triumph, but I need another one for tonight. He is taking me to dinner."
"What?" She burst out laughing. "We need coffee and a chat. You got time?"
"Of course," I said.
"I will just get a fresh pot. Hold that thought girl."
Naomi was my closest friend. We met at university, she studied Art and Design and me English of course. We hit it off from the word go and from then on, we were inseparable. Naomi knew me better than I knew myself sometimes and she was always there, even through my dark days and there had been a few of those over the years. I knew that I could trust her with anything and she in turn could trust me. I looked at a few of her sketches as I waited for her. They looked amazing; she was so talented. Naomi was just starting to hit the big time after a lot of years of hard work. Some soap actresses had worn her designs at a red-carpet event and now she had been inundated with requests. I was happy for her if anyone deserved success it was her. She

finally returned with a fresh pot of coffee and two cups. We waited until she had poured them out before she sat opposite me and looked at me pointedly. "So? Spill the beans, Miss James."

"He's invited me to dinner and he's picking me up at 2pm."

"Whoa there girly. What about last night? Did you meet his friends?"

"I did and they are both so nice and so handsome. Eduardo is dark like Xavier but with deep brown eyes and Gabe has like dark blonde hair with these most piercing green eyes."

Naomi sipped her coffee and smiled at me over the rim of her cup "They sound hunky. So, tell me about Xavier. Have you kissed him again?"

I closed my eyes and could feel the tinge of embarrassment tint my cheeks. "Yes."

"Oh my God!" she squealed. "And now he wants to take you for dinner?"

"Seems that way," I sighed. "And so, I have to tell him everything."

Naomi looks at me her lips in a line. "Even about Paris?"

The only other person who knew about what happened in Paris was Naomi. I had revealed everything to her following a double date that we went on when neither of us had really vibed with our dates and so we had ditched them as kindly as we could and then proceeded to get thoroughly drunk at a club and I had ended up telling her everything. Like the good friend she was, she thought it sexy and daring and especially as it involved one of the most eligible bachelors around.

"Yes, especially about Paris. How could I not? It has felt so awkward withholding talking to him about that night. I am sure that he did not know that the woman behind the mask was me and why would he?"

Naomi raised her eyebrows. "Complete coincidence that he happened to walk in that club on the night you were there…absolute destiny."

I raised my eyebrows at that anecdote. "Naomi…you and this destiny thing."

"Don't be so sceptical Alyssa. How else would you explain how you two met and then after walking away from the café you met

After Paris

again in rather strange circumstances. Pure destiny."
"And now I am writing a story on him."
"How's that coming along by the way?"
"Good. He is still holding back though. Seemingly telling me everything and yet not really telling me anything at all."
"Do you think he will?"
"I am planning to get him to open up to me today. I am going to have to tread carefully because whatever he has hidden, he is determined to keep it that way."
Naomi grinned wickedly. "Perhaps a bit of pillow talk?"
I laughed. "Naomi! I would never use what he told me in confidence in a story. You know me. I am not kiss and tell."
"I know, I know. How are you going to tell him about Theo?" She leaned forward full of concern. She knew that even the mere mention of that name gave me the jitters.
I let out a huge breath of air that I wasn't aware of holding.
"Just straight out. The funny thing is I think he may know Theo. They went to the same school. I found that out as I was doing my research the other day. Shit. I hope he doesn't know him."
"Awks babe," She grimaced pulling a face. "What are the chances of that happening? God, even you couldn't write this stuff."
"I know. But I need to tell him."
She held up her coffee cup. "A toast to the truth and whatever that may bring."
I raised my cup to hers and my stomach churned with nerves. I had no idea how Xavier was going to react to any of my revelations tonight. I just hoped he could see past it all and understand.
Naomi reached across the table and squeezed my hand. She knew this was a big deal for me.
"When you have finished that coffee, I will show you the dress I have in mind for you tonight. If after telling him you go down, at least it will be in flames."
I laughed but it sounded shallow even to my own ears. I didn't want it to go down badly. I wanted him to realise I had told him everything so that there were no secrets between us. I would be exposing my fears and, for the first time in ages, opening my heart. But would he be the same with me?

Xavier

I have pulled out all the stops for tonight.
She was worth it.
I know she told me not to wine and dine her, but I am going to wine and dine her like she has never been wined and dined before. For some reason I want to impress her, and I hope what I have planned is going to do just that.
I picked up my phone and tapped out a text to her.

Change of plan. Bring an overnight bag and your passport. See you at 2pm.

I waited a couple of minutes and then saw the three dots as she read my message and that she is typing back.

Seriously? Are you kidding?

I smirked and tapped my reply.

Never been more serious. Remember I am on a promise…

I sat back in my chair and for the first time in ages I didn't feel like doing any work. It was nearly lunchtime anyway and I was contemplating ringing through to Estelle and telling her I was going to take the rest of the day off when I heard my phone ping. I turned it over and my heart plummeted.

Sorry I can't. I must be somewhere tomorrow…early.

What? Shit? All my best laid plans gone up in smoke. Shit, shit, shit, shit. I heard the ping again and looked down.

Kidding. Would have loved to have seen your face Mr. Overly Confident!

I felt the grin tugging at my lips and then I sat back and laughed.

After Paris

God, this woman…and this is why I liked her. Yes, I liked her. As well as wanting to fuck her into next week, I really liked her. In just under a week, I felt closer to her than I had any other woman…how the hell had that happened? She was witty and funny as well as being as sexy as fuck. But she has something to tell me. She seemed so serious about what she must tell me that I am not going to lie, it is beginning to concern me a bit. I have searched her obviously but nothing strange came up. But going from experience I know that things can be kept hidden if you know the right people and she is a journalist and so would know who to speak to if she wanted something not to show up on social media. So, what is this 'thing' she must tell me? Last night I was so close to taking her back to my place and making her mine, totally and irrefutably but something held me back. For some reason I wanted her to come to me, wanted her to want me as much as I wanted her. I knew she was attracted to me by the way she kissed me back so full of longing and promise, but in a strange turnabout I was the one doing the chasing and she was the one evading me.

My mobile rang in my hand, for a moment I thought it would be Alyssa, but the name '*Maman*' lit up on the screen. I took a deep breath and answered.

"*Maman*," I smiled as I slipped into French easily. "How are you?"

"I am good Xavier. How's London?"

"Buzzing as usual. How is it in Monaco?"

"Oh darling, you know how it is here. Things change but everything stays the same."

"Any news to tell me?"

I heard her snort, a chic French snort but, nevertheless.

"Nothing that you would be interested in my boy."

I toyed with the idea of telling her about the article, about Alyssa but swiftly decided not to. My mother didn't act for a living anymore but that didn't stop the dramatics coming out every now and then. She knew I hated it, but she just didn't seem to be able to help herself.

"How's Henri?" I asked, knowing I was treading on thin ice. My mother was still a very attractive woman and she had had many a beau over the years. The latest was Henri, a very distinguished wine merchant who had been in and out of my mother's life for the last three years. My mother pretended that she really wasn't bothered if Henri was around or not, but I knew differently and knew she was extremely fond of him, although she would never admit it in a million years.

"He's ok I guess…who cares really? You know how it is with me and Henri. If he's around then that's fine if he's not, then that's fine too."

"You are such an actress," I laughed. "I really don't know who you are trying to fool with that act, but it doesn't wash with me, and you know Henri thinks it's a bag of bullshit too."

"Darling!" she feigned shock at my words. "How can you speak to your very own mother like this?"

"Why don't you just make an honest man of him *maman* and get it over with?"

"Xavier! Have you been drinking? So early in London too. Have you taken leave of your senses?"

I laughed again. "I am not drunk." *Just happy, happy at the thought of spending an evening with Alyssa.*

"Those English drink too much," My mother said in a disgusted tone. "I knew you would get into bad ways going to London."

"I am not drunk," I repeated and couldn't help rolling my eyes, even though she couldn't see me.

"Have you seen your father?" My mother threw in randomly.

"Why would I see him? Just because we both live in England. You know England is quite a big place, right?"

"He hasn't called you?"

"Again, why would he?" I felt myself getting defensive. I hadn't seen my father for about ten years, and that had been by accident. I was at some event and slowly getting drunk at the bar with Eduardo and Gabe when Eduardo suddenly stopped the conversation dead, staring over my shoulder. I turned to follow his gaze and come face to face with my father. He looked older but still handsome and distinguished with his full head of dark hair, so like my own, now sliced with silver at the temples. He was dressed impeccably, as always, and he had eyed me distastefully with those piercing blue eyes, that I also inherited,

After Paris

not missing a thing and then said my name "Xavier."
I had sobered up pretty quickly and swallowed down the sick feeling that had washed over me. "Father."
"Are you well?"
"Yes, thank you. Are you?"
"As well as to be expected. I hear through the grapevine you are making quite a killing on the stock market."
"I am doing ok."
"Excellent. Glad you are doing so well. How's Mirabelle?"
I shrugged. "Oh, you know her, yes or course you do. She was your wife. What I mean is, she's well." *Well done. Stupid fucking answer. Why did he always make me feel like I am thirteen again?*
We had stared at each other in silence for a few moments.
"Good. Well, nice to see you, Xavier. Look after yourself." And then he had turned and disappeared into the crowd of people.
At the time I had been too stunned to reply and so I had watched him go in silence, embarrassed and humiliated that my own father had just spoken to me like some acquaintance that he had bumped into. Eduardo and Gabe stood behind me, both as stunned and silent as me. Ed had laid a consolatory hand on my shoulder. There was no need to say anything. My heart had splintered that day.
"Xavier," My mother's voice cut into my thoughts. "You need to settle this thing between you. Please go and try to see him…"
"No!" I snapped and then regained my sense of calm, and I repeated it much more in control. "No *maman*. He knows where I am if he wants to see me."
"Stubborn! Both of you."
"Well, I wonder where I got that trait from?"
"Definitely not from me."
I laughed. "I guess you would say I just got my suave sophisticated French charm from you?"
I heard her husky laugh. "Well darling, I don't mind taking that accolade. When are you coming to see me?"
"I'll try to come and see you soon," I promised and the thought of taking Alyssa to meet my mother materialised out of nowhere. I had never taken any woman to meet my mother. I shook my head slightly to dispel that idea.

"*À bientôt* my darling boy. I need to go and prepare for yet another soiree this evening."

I smiled. My mother always pretended that she hated going to these events but secretly she loved it and loved to have her still adoring fans fawning over her.

"Have a lovely evening."

"Yes darling...and if you could just push some of that stubbornness aside..."

"Bye *maman*." I pressed the button to end the call and let out a huge sigh. She never gave up hope, unlike me who had given up any hope of having a relationship with my father years ago. I suppose at some point Alyssa was going to delve into questions about my father. So far, she had only skirted around the subject, but I knew she was curious and was saving the deeper questioning for tonight. I knew it was coming and yet I still hadn't decided just how much I was going to divulge. I had learnt a lot over the years where journalists were concerned and most of the time important serious things were best left unsaid but somehow, I trusted her and knew that if I asked for something not to be spoken about, she would respect that. My relationship with Nicholas Montgomery was complicated and marred by tragedy and it was not easy to talk about him or the circumstances of our estrangement. I let out a heavy sigh. There was no way I was reaching out to my father, not now and maybe not ever and despite everything that had happened, that thought still saddened me.

I looked at my watch, ironically a present from my father on my thirteenth birthday when everything was good and my father loved me enough to pass on to me his Patek Phillippe watch, which was a present to him from his father at the same age. I loved this watch and wore it almost every day. I had it serviced and cleaned once a year and I knew the only time I would part with it was when or if I had a son in the future and just my father had done, I would pass it to him on his thirteenth birthday. I touched the smooth face, marvelling at the perfection of the timepiece and again that feeling of sadness descended, like a grey cloud hanging over me. I snapped back to the present and

After Paris

decided that I would leave early. I gathered my things together and closed my screen. Work could wait for a change. I had a good team in place, and they could run the show for the afternoon. Estelle looked up in surprise as I stopped in front of her desk.
"I'm leaving for the weekend Estelle. I don't want you to stay all afternoon either. Please go home at lunchtime."
"Are you sure Mr. Montgomery?"
She was such a sweet girl and very conscientious. "Yes Estelle. I insist. Have a good weekend."
"Thank you, Mr. Montgomery. You too."
I smiled to myself as I waited for the lift. I fully intended to have the best weekend ever.

I picked Alyssa up at her house. Pulling a small case behind her, she came out dressed in blue jeans and a baggy pink sweater and I don't think I have ever wanted her so much as I did at that moment. She looked just as beautiful as she had in that red dress last night and that had just about blown my mind. I deserved some kind of award for not seducing her into my bed so far, but tonight there was no more holding back. She slid into the back seat next to me as my driver put her luggage into the boot. She smelled of flowers and she looked good enough to eat. As the car glided into the London traffic, I reached out and took her hand in mine and rested it on my lap. She looked at me questionably and I met her eyes with a grin. "What?"
"Holding my hand?"
I laughed. Yes, it was normally totally outside of my comfort zone, but here and now with her it felt right. "Call me old fashioned," I grinned at her. "Do you not want us to hold hands?"
She shook her head. "Oh no. I like it, but just didn't expect it that's all."
I squeezed her fingers in response.
"So where are you whisking me off to? Why do I need my passport?"
I smiled. "Now that would be telling."
"I am not good at surprises…"
"Well, you are going to have to be with me. I like surprising

people."
She laughed. "How was work today?"
"I don't know. I played hooky."
She stared at me incredulous. "Really? Now *that* has surprised me."
"Found I had other things on my mind."
"Oh yeah? Like what?" She asked and her voice had dropped an octave giving it a kind of breathless sexy quality.
I leaned towards her and whispered in her ear. "Like you…*sans vêtements*…"
"What does it mean? What I remember from my school French '*sans*' is 'without' and '*vêtements*' is …. oh…" I watched her face colour slightly as she figured out what I had said. *Without clothes.*
I let my smile stretch slowly upon my lips. "Getting the idea?" I whispered.
Her eyes stared into mine and then flicked to Anton, my driver. "I pay him not to listen," I added as I took moment to smell her hair. Yes, ok I was guilty of it. Her hair smelt amazing.
Her huge dark eyes turned to mine, and our lips were only inches away from each other. I wanted to kiss her, kiss her like she had never been kissed before, break down all her defences and make her beg me to take her. With all of the will power I could muster I moved back in my seat and looked out of the window because if I looked at her now, I would cave in and kiss her and never stop.
We remained silent for a while, perhaps because she, like me, could only think of us naked together in a queen-sized hotel bed with her writhing and begging me for more as I thrust inside her again and again. Her soft voice interrupted my over excited thoughts. "Are we going to City Airport?"
"I should have blindfolded you," I grinned and was only half joking. The image of Alyssa blindfolded and at my mercy sent signals straight to my cock and I had to bite back a moan as I felt myself immediately harden.
"Xavier, where are we going?"
"Well, it was going to be a surprise, but I thought we could fly to Paris."

CHAPTER TEN

Paris

Alyssa

Oh hell!! Paris? Shit, shit, shit. I forced an excited smile on my face. Why would I not be excited right? I should be. A hot, handsome, half French, half God, beautiful specimen of a man is taking me to the city of love and all I can think is shit!

"So," he said as I swallowed my nerves and smiled at him. "I thought I would take you back to Paris and take you to dinner. Like I wanted to that first time we met."

I exhaled a huge breath. "How romantic of you."

He smiled catching the mocking tone in my voice. "Is it too much Miss James?"

I shrugged my shoulders and shook my head. Under normal circumstances with no memories, it would be perfect. I closed my eyes to gather my thoughts. What better place to tell him right? About that night about the mysterious masked woman with the butterfly tattoo in the city where we met, where we shared so much more than a coffee and a chat outside a busy little pavement café. I opened my eyes and stared out of the window, the nerves fluttering about in my stomach again. He squeezed my hand, and I turned my eyes to look at him.

"What?" he asked as he shook his head slightly, questioning me. There it was again…the connection between us. He was so in tune with me. "Did I…I mean have I overstepped the mark?"

I saw the uncertainty in his eyes, and I shook my head suddenly ashamed that I was ruining a beautiful moment. What did it matter where I told him? I just had to tell him.
I squeezed his fingers back. "No. I was just overwhelmed for the moment that you would think of such a lovely thing to do."
He grinned. "Yeah, I'm not really one for romantic gestures but somehow it seemed right for this occasion. I'm pulling out all the stops here Alyssa. I know you are not easily impressed, and I know you think I am some sort of playboy and I suppose whisking you to dinner in Paris is not helping my cause, but I have never done this before, not for any woman ever. I just wanted you to know that."
I looked at him. He seemed genuine and I believed him. Through my work I had got good at reading people over the years, and it was easy to spot the fakes. For some reason this man was placing me apart from all the other women he had had in his life, making me special and suddenly I was scared, scared I was not going to live up to his expectations, scared that when he knew the truth, he would be disappointed and realise that I was just like everyone else. Flawed and a tiny bit broken.
I forced a smile to my lips. "You know I still have to finish our interview, right?"
He raised an eyebrow. "Yes, I know, but it doesn't all have to be work does it? The moment will come when the work stops, and you are just you and I am just me."
I knew exactly what he meant, and it made my heart beat just that little bit faster. What was between us was not just the interview, it was so much more, and we both knew it.
I glanced out of the window and noted that we were driving onto the actual tarmac on the airport where a sleek, shiny private jet awaited with two cabin crew at the bottom of the steps leading onto the plane. The car stopped and the driver jumped out and opened the door for me. I slid out reluctantly letting go of Xavier's hand, but he was right behind me, and his hand reached out and took my hand again, entwining his fingers with mine.
"You have got to be kidding me," I whispered as he walked me towards the plane. "A private jet? You really have pulled out all the stops."

After Paris

He grinned. "It's the company jet, not mine personally."
I rolled my eyes. "Oh well that's ok then."
He squeezed my hand. "Please tell me you are just a little bit impressed now?"
"What? I travel by private jet all the time. Nothing new here Mr. Montgomery."
He laughed. "God, you are hard work. What does a guy have to do?"
I smiled and felt a small excitement bomb explode through my body. Being treated like this was wonderful and although I had acted all cool and nonchalant, I had, of course, never been on a private jet before. I rolled my lips together to try and stop the huge grin that threatened to spread across my lips. This beautiful man was really going all out to impress me, and the thing was although I knew this was all totally normal to him, I had been more impressed by what I had found out the evening before, the children's hospital wing that he had almost funded himself, the work on the playground, the charity events that raised thousands for under privileged. However, it was a thrill to hear him say that he had never done this for any other woman in his past.
I stopped just before we got to the steps, and he turned to look at me. "Seriously Xavier. This is amazing. Thank you."
He raised his eyebrows. "Why do I always get the impression that you are taking the piss out of me?"
I loved his retort; it showed me he wasn't taking all of this too seriously at all and for a split second he looked so vulnerable. I couldn't resist and leant up and kissed his lips softly. The feel of his lips on mine was divine as he kissed me back and as I pulled away, I looked up in his eyes and saw the surprise. He hadn't expected that, and I was glad that I could surprise Mr. Cool as a cucumber.
"Are you going to show me this plane or not?" I whispered.
He smiled and brought my fingers to his lips grazing them over my knuckles. *Shit that was sexy.* "Of course, Miss James."
The plane was as luxurious and as comfortable as I imagined it would be all cream leather seats and elegance. The hostess served champagne in tall slim flutes as Xavier, and I sat opposite each other with a shiny walnut table between us. We clinked glasses

and I took a sip of my champagne.

"May I suggest that you try and control the amount of that stuff you consume this time?" Xavier grinned at me. "I don't want you to be tipsy for our dinner tonight."

I grinned back. "Don't worry. I have learnt my lesson. Only one glass for me as it would be rude not to. Plus, I need to keep my head for the questions I am going to ask you."

He smiled but I noted the concern that briefly clouded his eyes. "Should I be worried about the subjects you are going to cover?"

I shook my head as the bubbles from my champagne went up my nose "Nothing you can't handle."

I took a sip of the bubbly stuff and watched him over the rim of my glass. "It is not my job to pry into your life Xavier, although I do want our readers to know a different side to you. I don't want to do the playboy angle, and I must admit that after getting to know you a bit better it now seems an injustice to you and all the work you do. Dare I say it, you are so much more than a pretty boy with a penchant for society beauties."

"Perhaps after you delve into my life a bit more you may find you actually prefer the playboy Xavier Montgomery," the smile is still around his full delectable lips but with an added tinge of sadness. "The more you find out, the deeper you dig, what you find may both shock and disappoint you."

I shook my head. "I don't think so. The real Xavier Montgomery could never disappoint me."

"Let's hope not."

This conversation had got a bit intense and so I smiled a megawatt smile. "So, Xavier Montgomery, where are you taking me for dinner tonight?"

"Surprise," he wriggled his eyebrows and I laughed.

"Can you at least tell me where we are staying?"

He nodded. "The only place to stay when you are in Paris, the George V."

I threw open the doors to the room and tried, really tried, not to be impressed but I couldn't not be. I went out onto the private terrace and took in the view of the Eiffel tower and just like that

After Paris

I felt any resolve I had left to resist Xavier, which was almost barely non-existent by now anyway, fly over the balcony railings and float away into the clear blue Parisian sky above me. I felt him behind me and when I turned, he was leaning against the door frame watching me with a smile on his face.
"I think I have finally impressed the girl," he said smoothly.
I laughed. "Yes, I think you just may have. Oh my God Xavier. This is just taking my breath away."
"Paris weaves a magical spell over one and all."
"And the room is amazing," I said, not sure how I felt that we had our own bedrooms. They were adjoining but even so. Had he changed his mind about us? About taking this further and sleeping together? I had fully planned to seduce him tonight. He may have pulled out all the stops with the location and the fancy dinner and the private plane, but I was going to pull out all the stops in the bedroom department. *I wanted him so badly.* I looked at him as he stared at me and thought for perhaps the millionth time that he was just the most handsome man I had ever seen. He was dressed casually today in tight faded blue jeans and a white linen shirt. He had been wearing a dark blue linen jacket but somehow that had got discarded along the way. His dark hair was ruffled and bit wild and his blue eyes were especially bright and piercing today and those eyelashes were almost indecent. Only men got those long dark eyelashes, which is so unfair. I suddenly had the urge to kiss him. I felt a stirring between my legs, being back in Paris had brought it all back to me. The way he had taken me that night, so forcibly against the wall and then the constant onslaught when we had finally made it to the bed. All night long, like he couldn't get enough of me. I had been sore for days afterwards and each time I felt the soreness I remembered him, and the want returned. I always wanted him. Even when I didn't want him, I wanted him. I closed my eyes and turned back to the view. I stared unseeing at the sights and sounds of the city of love and all I could feel was the presence of the man behind me.
"Thought I would have shower," he said his voice a tad deeper and huskier than a few moments ago.
"Ok," I answered not turning around. "Think I may just stand

here for a while taking in the atmosphere. What time is dinner?"
"7.30. Is that ok for you?"
"Fine. I will be ready."
"Alyssa…"
I closed my eyes. Even the way he said my name made me melt. I steeled myself and turned.
"I did the right thing didn't I? Bringing us to Paris?"
I nodded. "Definitely."
He nodded and then turned and went back into the suite.
I waited for him in his room. I could hear the shower running and I was so tempted to go in, strip off and join him, but things still needed to be said first and I had finally built up the courage to tell him at least one part of my past. The water stopped and I took a deep breath as he came out of the bathroom with his hair wet and a small towel wrapped around his waist, he stopped dead when he saw me, and I held my breath. He looked like a model, all lean lines, six pack and smooth tanned skin and I really wished we had already talked, and I could just get naked with him and put this baby to bed, but instead I smiled up at him.
"We need to talk," I said my voice coming out a lot huskier than I thought it would.
He pushed his hands through his hair, sleeking his hair back from his face. "Am I going to be devastated by this revelation?"
"I hope not," I said and tried to ignore the hard muscly chest as he walked towards me and sat next to me on the bed.
"I have already told you Alyssa, nothing you say will change what I think about you."
"But it might."
He put a fingertip to my lips. "It won't. So, tell me."
I took another deep breath. "I…the thing is…last year I almost got married." I looked at him and the only thing that changed was an eyebrow raised as he waited for me to carry on. "I stood him up at the altar. Not something I am proud of, but I couldn't go through with it."
He remained silent but took my hand and entwined his fingers with mine. "Ok, go on."
"Theo was manipulative and dominating. He started off being the sweetest man ever but soon became someone I didn't

After Paris

particularly like. It was very subtle at the beginning, making out he had planned something for us when he knew I had made other plans with friends or colleagues, and I found it flattering that he wanted to be with me so much but then I noticed that it happened all the time. He really didn't want me going out anywhere unless it was with him. Then he wanted me to move in with him. I didn't want to, it was much too soon, but he was relentless. Luckily, I did have the sense not to sell my house, as he had suggested, but to rent it out just to see how it panned out with him. To be honest, I was already having my doubts and hated the way he always managed to get around things when I felt hemmed in or claustrophobic by his behaviour."

I looked at Xavier and his eyes had turned midnight blue. He was trying to control his anger, but I saw the glint in his eyes as they narrowed and the expression on his face hardened.

"As you know I am quite headstrong and opinionated but somehow over the months I was with him he managed to quash any idea or thought that I had. Sometimes he did it in front of friends too, made fun of my opinion like I had no idea of what I was talking about. In the end I just didn't offer any opinion on anything, I just stopped joining in and stood like some dumb idiot smiling innately while he held court with our circle of friends. He proposed to me at a family dinner with his parents and siblings. I am ashamed to say that I didn't have the balls to say no in front of them. It was just assumed I would marry him…I mean why would I not want to…. he was the perfect man. Good looking, rich, destined to take over his family shipping business. Why on earth would I not want to marry him? But I didn't. And the more I felt oppressed by his behaviour and our relationship the more I clammed up. Before I knew it, I was picking out wedding dresses with this mum and sister, booking venues for the wedding reception and generally being railroaded into a wedding and a marriage with a man I was not in love with and did not want to be with."

Xavier stood up abruptly and racked his finger through his hair. I knew he was getting angry as he paced up and down in front of me letting out deep breaths as he walked.

"Fuck Alyssa. What the honest fuck? I am getting fucking images

of strangling this guy. Did he ever hit you? Please tell me no because then I really would have to find him and beat the shit out of him."
I shook my head. "No. He was never physically abusive. Just psychologically. But really that is just as bad, isn't it?"
"Yes! Maybe I still will beat the shit out of him!"
A burst of nervous laughter erupted from me even though nothing being said was funny. I covered my face with my hands and felt Xavier lean down in front of me as he gently pulled my hands away from my face. Hot tears were in my eyes. Tears of anger for letting myself get caught up in something so negative and wrong.
"Alyssa, this wasn't your fault, ok? No man should treat someone like he treated you."
"But why did I put up with his shit?" I asked through my tears. "It was so unlike me, I hated how he made me feel, hated the way he manipulated my life."
"He sounds like a bully. That is what bullies do," Xavier said wiping away my tears with the pad of his thumb. "So, you stood him up at the altar huh?"
I nodded. "Yes. I was there. In my beautiful wedding dress bought and paid for by his family and I just couldn't do it. I couldn't say yes when the priest asked me. Theo even tried to answer for me, but the priest said that I had to answer. My answer was no. I fled. I could hear all the shouting behind me of Theo calling me names and shouting obscenities, but I just kept running and didn't stop until I was back at the hotel and getting my stuff and running away."
"You did the right thing," Xavier smiled. "Where did you run to?"
I lifted my eyes to his. "Paris."

CHAPTER ELEVEN

Xavier

Oh Fuck! I had brought her back to the place where she had run to. Now I understood her expression that she valiantly tried to mask when I said where we were going. I had thought that she was just trying to prove she was not impressed, but now it all made sense.

"Do you want to leave Alyssa? I can have the jet ready in an hour to fly us back to London?"

She shook her head. "No, please don't. I love it here. It was my sanctuary for a while. I love being here with you."

"Are you sure? Does it not give you bad memories?"

She shook her head again with a sad smile turning up the corners of her full cupid bow lips. "No, quite the opposite in fact."

"Ok. If you are sure," I sat down on the bed beside her again and wrapped an arm around her shoulders. I never did this with women. Usually, I fucked them slow and got rid of them fast. There was none of this 'touchy feely' stuff. But Alyssa was not like the other women I had met. Alyssa was…. well Alyssa.

"So, what happened afterwards? Did he run after you and try and talk you around?"

"No. He cut all ties with me. He threw my stuff out of his apartment. He told our friends that I had been cheating on him and had run off with my lover. He turned it all around so that he became the victim, and I became the bad guy. He trolled me on social media. Wrote hateful disgusting things about me and constantly bombarded me with threatening emails and messages until I turned off my phone and bought a new one here in Paris. He said I had humiliated him."

I snorted a laugh. "What an arsehole."

"I got solicitors letters from his family saying that I owed them money for the wedding, even though I had never wanted any of the things they had arranged. My parents ended up bailing me out just to get them off my back. It was awful."

I squeezed her hand. "That must have been terrible. Who is this guy, Alyssa? You don't have to tell me if you don't want to."

She closed her eyes and when she opened them again, I saw how nervous she was.

"That's just it. Xavier, I think you may know him...when I was doing the research on you for the interview I realised that you had gone to the same school."

I frowned trying to remember a Theo at school. The only one I could remember was that little shit head in the year below me. "Theo? Theo who? What was his surname?"

"Constantine," she whispered. "Theo Constantine."

And it all came flooding back to me. Theo Constantine *was* the shit head in the year below me at school. He was a bully then and obviously was still a bully now. There were times at school when I should have kicked his arse, but by then I was a prefect and Head Boy and couldn't get myself into scrapes with other students. My father was already waiting to pull me over the coals for plenty of other stuff and I couldn't mess up being Head Boy too. Plenty of times I had given Theo Constantine verbal warnings about his behaviour and once I remembered I had taken him by the scruff of his neck and pushed him up against the wall when I had witnessed him being particularly nasty to another pupil. Luckily Eduardo and Gabe had talked me out of giving him a good beating, although both agreed that he thoroughly deserved it. I remembered the smirk on that plastic good looking face of his and the feeling I had had of wanting to smack it off.

After Paris

"I hated him at school Alyssa. He was in the year below me and he was a bully then, a very clever bully but I saw him for all he was. Fuck, I wish I had punched him then."

She smiled but remained silent. God, this must have been a nightmare for her. Why on earth had she ever got embroiled with that shit head? Then I had a horrible thought. She must have slept with him. There was no way an arsehole like Theo was having a woman like Alyssa and not sleeping with her. I felt sick. I stood up again and saw the hesitant look in her eyes. She wasn't sure what I was going to say next.

"Did he...did he hurt you in bed Alyssa?"

She closed her eyes and for a moment I thought she wasn't going to answer but then she said "No...not hurt as such...he was rough...sometimes I zoned out when he was...anyway it was never as it should be. I am sure that he had other women. Women more attuned to his preferences. He often said I was too vanilla for him. A few times he called me frigid. I am not by the way...frigid that is..."

God, I hated that bastard. I pushed away all the torturous images I had in my mind of him and her together and forced a smile to my lips. "I am sure you're not Alyssa."

I heard her sigh and sat down again next to her and pulled her to me kissing her hair which smelt of lemons. "I am so sorry for how he treated you, Alyssa. Thank God you are strong and have your own mind. You should never change for anyone. He is a complete and utter bastard. Thank you for telling me. It must have been hard for you to open up like that."

She nodded against my chest and my hatred for Theo Fucking Constantine compounded by like a hundred thousand percent. I wanted to mess him up and mess him up bad. I decided to get Ed and Gabe onto him, find out who he did business with. Maybe if I couldn't physically punch him, I could hurt him in other ways.

"Why don't you go and have a nice bath and relax before tonight?" I said against her hair.

She nodded again. "Yes, that's a good idea. There is something else I need to tell you though..."

My mobile rang at that precise moment. I looked behind me on the bed. It was Ed. Good no time like the present. I would get him to find out what he could on that bastard.

"Can you tell me after honey? I need to get this. I do want to know so just hold that thought for a moment, ok?"

She stood up and walked towards her room. "OK, I am going to draw my bath."

I nodded and smiled and then waited until she was in her room before grabbing my phone and swiping to answer.

"Hey buddy, we have a situation we need to sort," I whispered.

When I had filled Ed in, he was incensed as I was and promised he would find out all he could on Theo Constantine. It wouldn't be hard. The Constantine's had a shipping business, not really my area of expertise or knowledge but I could still stir the waters and make them muddy if I needed to. I padded through into Alyssa's room. I could hear her singing in the bath, and it made me smile. I had deliberately booked this suite with two rooms as I didn't want her to feel pressured into sleeping with me and after what she had just told me, it seemed like for once I had done the right thing. I wanted her to want me, not be pressured because I had booked us the same room. Hopefully tonight after dinner, she would come to me. I pushed open her bathroom door. She was up to her neck in bath bubbles and had her pods in her ears, her head bobbing in time with whatever music she was listening to. Her eyes were closed. There was nothing I wanted more at this moment than to strip off and get in the bath with her but that was not going to happen. Try telling my cock that though. He was hard and standing to attention. Thank God I had changed into some grey sweatpants. It was a bit easier to disguise than if I just had that towel around me still.

She opened her eyes and when she saw me there, she smiled. She took one of the earphones out. "How long you been standing there? Please don't tell me you heard me singing?"

"Your singing was great."

She sighed and blew out her cheeks in exasperation. "Liar! I am the worst singer. Oh shit!"

"Alyssa, nothing you have done or said has made me feel any different. Not even the singing."

After Paris

"Really?"

I nodded. "Yes, really."

"Why don't you come over here?" she asked her voice going all soft and husky, which of course my cock heard straight away. It was painful now as it was so hard.

"Because, if I come any closer things will get kind of wild...and I can't promise that we will get to dinner..."

She smiled some more. "So, you still want me then...I mean still want to...." Her voice trailed off as she looked at me with those huge brown eyes. "I thought maybe you had changed your mind as you booked me my own room, and now you know about Theo..."

"Alyssa. I still want you. Painfully so, believe me. I only booked your own room as I didn't want you to feel pressured. And I don't think we should mention that name again tonight or any other night."

She smiled. "Just for your information, I don't feel pressured at all."

"Good," I smiled back as I leant against the door jamb. "But if I stand here any longer, I will feel the pressure and the need to come over there and get in that water with you and so I am going to my room to send some quick emails instead and try and get my body and my mind back onto neutral ground."

She sat up and I could see the tops of her full buoyant breasts just beneath the bubbles. I groaned.

"Are you trying to kill me or what?" I laughed as I turned away and walked back to my room with the biggest erection ever.

"You can run Mr. Montgomery," she called after me. "But I will catch you sooner or later."

Catch me baby? No need to catch me. I will not be running anywhere later believe me.

Alyssa

The knock on my door startled me. I had been getting ready for dinner and was so wrapped up in my thoughts that I had almost forgotten that Xavier was in the next room. I couldn't of course. Forget he was there that is. I could feel his presence like a huge magnet pulling me towards him. I stared at my reflection in the mirror. Naomi had been so right choosing this dress for me for dinner tonight. It was perfect, like it had been made for me. Black, simple contour loving shift dress down to just above my knees with a low V neck showing off my boobs to perfection. Naomi had had to find me a special bra to wear with it. The sleeves were long and made of pleated chiffon and were tight at the cuff. It was an amazing dress and made me feel like someone else wearing it…. like the girl with the tattoo. My stockings were black and very sheer, and my shoes were black suede and high.

"Alyssa, are you ready? The car is downstairs waiting." Xavier called through the door.

"Two minutes," I called back applying another layer of my favourite red lipstick. Then with a last fluff of my hair I grabbed my clutch and pushed my lipstick inside. I was going to have to do. I opened the door, and he was standing just outside. He looked so handsome in a black suit and white shirt open at the neck, that for a moment I was speechless. He likewise as his eyes roamed over my body from my shoes right up to my eyes. I saw him check out my boobs and from the look on his face it was evident that he liked what he saw.

"Do I look ok?" I asked my voice faltering a bit as I imagined him saying to forget dinner as he ripped my dress off and slammed me against the wall.

"More than ok," he breathed, and his voice was all husky and sexy and made me squirm a bit from the want and need I felt in the southern region of my body. "Fuck Alyssa. You really are trying to kill me, aren't you?"

I laughed. "That wasn't my intention…no."

"Just so you know I will be hard all night sitting near you with that dress on and looking like you do."

His words thrilled me. I loved knowing that Xavier Montgomery had an erection as big as the Eiffel Tower itself in his very well-cut trousers because of me.

I laughed again and took his outstretched hand. As soon as we touched, I felt it. The connection.

After Paris

"Oh, hold on a minute," I said pulling my hand reluctantly from his. "I forgot my notebook and pen."
I rushed back into my room and found my trusty notebook and grabbed it. Tonight, I was aiming to fill this notebook with all he had to tell me. Hopefully it would be all I needed as I was trying hard not to be too biased with my writing. The more I found out about him, the more I just wanted to keep to myself. I found I didn't want to share Xavier with the world. I wanted to get this interview over and done with so that we could concentrate on us…and just us.

The car ride was fraught with an intensity that neither of us could deny. He obviously wanted me, and I obviously wanted him and yet here we were going through a dinner so that I could get the last information out of him before I could finish my work. I looked out of the window as the streets and landmarks of Paris whisked past my eyes in a blur and tried to ignore the feeling of his hand in mine on the seat between us.
He squeezed my fingers and I turned to look at him. "Are you ok?"
"Yes. I am. This is exciting. I suppose you are not going to tell me where we are going?"
"Nope."
I sighed and smiled. "You love a surprise, don't you?"
"I love to surprise you yes."
"Not even a hint?"
He shook his head. "You couldn't even kiss it out of me."
I raised a suggestive eyebrow. "Oooh, shall I try that?"
He laughed. "If you did you would never know, because we would never get there." He looked out of the window. "Anyway, we are almost there now."
A few minutes later the car pulled over to the kerb and the driver jumped out to open the door. I slid out and stood on the pavement whilst Xavier chatted to the driver in French and then he joined me on the pavement. He took my hand and led me inside what seemed to be another hotel. We walked through the lobby and then stopped outside what appeared to be huge, elegant dining room.

The maître'd appeared from nowhere and smiled at both of us. "Monsieur Montgomery et Mademoiselle. Welcome to Epicure. Your room is ready. Please follow me."
"Our room?" I whispered to Xavier as we made our way through the main dining room, and I took in the elegant dining couples at the equally elegant tables. I saw the women at the tables glance up at him with obvious interest and I gripped his hand just that little bit tighter.
Not tonight madams et mademoiselles, tonight he is mine.
"Trust me," he whispered back.
The maître'd pushed open a double set of doors which led into a private dining room set up for two. It was beautiful. I was in complete awe. I could not believe that Xavier Montgomery had gone through all this trouble for me. Two waiters stood on each side of the table waiting to pull our chairs out for us. We sat down and the maître'd passed Xavier the wine list as the waiters poured some water for both of us. And then we were alone. They disappeared through the double doors silently.
"Holy shit!" I whispered.
Xavier hid a smile. "Do not tell me I have managed to impress you twice today?"
"If I said I wasn't impressed I would be lying, this is beyond amazing."
"Just wait until you taste the food. It is perfection on a plate. They have three Michelin stars. I have only ever brought one other woman here, my mother."
I sat there speechless for a while absorbing the atmosphere as Xavier studied the wine list.
"Do you prefer red or white?" He asked looking across the table at me.
"White, I think. Something light, fruity. I don't know. I trust your judgement on this." I picked up the gold gilded menu in front of me and each course looked beautiful. It was all in French and so I would need Xavier's help. When I looked up, he was watching me with a strange look on his face.
"What?" I whispered.
"You don't have to whisper," he laughed and then leant forward, his elbows resting on the table. "I was just thinking, you should

After Paris

be on the menu. And that led my mind to other things…like you bent over this table, your dress pushed up around your waist and no underwear on…."

Oh. My. God. This man can talk dirty, usually I would be shocked but somehow when it came out of Xavier's mouth it was just sexy and inviting. I sat back in my chair and took a nervous sip of water.

"And where are you?" I asked boldly.

"Between your legs, looking at you…tasting you…"

There was a discreet knock at the door and with amused eyes on me, Xavier called for them to enter and then ordered the wine. With just words he had rendered me useless. My nipples were hard in my bra. My insides were mush. Between my legs was molten liquid. I had to concentrate on something else and got note pad and my phone ready.

"Would you like me to order food for you?"

I nodded not even trusting myself to speak.

He smirked. "Anything you don't like?"

"Baked Beans," I grinned. "And capers."

His laugh was soft, and I loved the sound of it. "Lucky for you there are no dishes here tonight with either of those things. Shall we just go for the scallops for starters, chicken for the main and dessert…. dessert I will leave up to you."

"Sounds wonderful," I smiled, purposely ignoring his sexy innuendo. *Get your mind back on work Alyssa.* "So, you bring your mother here. What was it like growing up with a famous actress as a mother?"

"I didn't know anything else. My mother had this job that meant she was always meeting other famous people, and everyone seemed to know who she was but to me she was just my mother."

"What was your relationship like?"

"Good. She wasn't around as much as I liked but she always made sure I was well looked after and when I could, I used to accompany her onto the film sets. I met Bridget Bardot when I was small apparently. I don't remember meeting her. My mother says Ms. Bardot thought I was cute."

I smiled. *Ms. Bardot would think you were even cuter now.*

"What about your father?"

I saw Xavier's eyes cloud over, just like they had the first time I had asked about his father. "I didn't see much of him after the age of thirteen when I was sent off to boarding school. He and my mother divorced the year after, and I would spend most of my holidays in France. He never asked to see me, and I was ok with that."
"Were you? Ok with that?"
He shrugged. "It was fine. My relationship with my father had always been strained at best and so it wasn't that much different. Except then it meant I couldn't disappoint him so much."
Alarm bells rang. Oh no. That's not good. Obviously, there were issues with his father. Shit.
The waiters arrived with the wine and poured for us. Xavier tasted it and nodded his approval. He then ordered the food and they disappeared again.
"I love it when you speak in French," I said, and my voice was all breathy. *What the hell?*
"Do you?" he asked sipping his wine, his eyes staring into mine. "Does it turn you on?"
I stared back at him. "Yes."
No need for elaboration. I took a sip of my wine and put the glass back on the table.
"Anyway, back to work, excellent wine by the way. So, you never see your father?"
"No."
"Is there no way you can repair your relationship?"
"No."
I pinched the bridge of my nose between my thumb and forefinger. "Are you going to reply to all of my questions in just one-word answers?"
"Perhaps," He sat back in his chair. "Seems to work for you when you are writing."
I wrote in my note pad.
"See," he accused. "I bet you only wrote one word."
I nodded "Yes, I did. Evasive."
"My father is a no-go subject. You can write in your interview that we are estranged and plan to stay that way."
I turned off my recorder. "What happened?"

After Paris

Xavier stared at me, but I knew he wasn't seeing me. He had shut off his mind to that line of questioning.

"Will you tell me one day? Not as Alyssa James journalist, but just as me Alyssa?"

He blinked and he looked at me. "Yes. Maybe. One day. Just not today."

I nodded and switched the recorder back on. "Do you prefer English women or French?"

He snorted a laugh. "Fuck, what sort of question is that?"

"A legitimate one," I laughed.

"There is only one answer obviously...English."

I grinned. "Right answer. French women have a habit of throwing things at you, don't they?"

He rolled his eyes. "Will you ever let me forget that?"

"No chance," I smiled glad that my stupid question had got him away from the subject of his father.

At that moment the starters arrived and looked delicious. They melted in the mouth. I was almost in ecstasy. By God the French knew a thing or two about cooking and I guess three Michelin star chefs knew more than most.

We chatted amicably as we ate. It was good. It felt comfortable. The food was superb, but the company was better. I don't know how it happened, but Xavier had moved his chair nearer to me during the meal and was now sitting next to me as opposed to opposite. I left the recording on as we chatted. It was good to get an insight as to the private Xavier too. I would never write about this, but it gave me as a writer, a more rounded holistic approach. He was entertaining, charming and was genuinely interested whenever I spoke.

"So, what about your parents?" he asked as we finished our mains, which were again out of this world.

"They live in Surrey in a semi-rural location. My dad is called Marcus, and he is a GP and I think he wanted me to become one too, but I always loved writing. I think I get it from my mum, Joanna. She has always encouraged me to write, she loves it herself and has had a few short stories published in magazines."

"Siblings?"

I shook my head. "No. Only child. Just like you."

That cloud appeared over his handsome face again. What the hell was this all about?

"Xavier?"

"It's nothing. Ignore me."

It obviously was something but again he probably was not going to share it with me here and now. "Did I say something wrong?" He shook his head. "No. You didn't say anything wrong." He forced a smile onto his lips. "So, dessert?"

I nodded. "I think so. Shall we share?"

"Good idea."

We ordered the poached pear with Chantilly ice cream and pecan something or other. I couldn't understand what was written or what was said but it sounded lovely. And we ordered coffee for afterwards.

The pear arrived and Xavier insisted on feeding me. He watched my mouth as I ate, and I could feel myself getting slowly turned on again. Everything he did was so sensual and when he licked some cream off the corner of my mouth, I almost bent over the table myself. Ignoring my weak protestations, he pulled me onto his lap, and it felt good being in his arms again. I wrapped my arms around his neck and entwined my fingers in his silky hair curling at the collar of his shirt.

"Xavier, what if the waiters come in?"

"They won't. I told them not to."

"What? So, they now know we are up to no good."

"They are French. They understand these things."

I laughed. "Sometimes I wish I was French."

He kissed my neck and I shivered.

"I like you just as you are" he whispered against my skin.

His lips were trailing over my skin, and I couldn't help but surrender. I let out a soft groan and he stopped and looked at me, his eyes all serious.

"Can you not groan like that? I can't resist when you do that."

"I can't help it. Don't kiss me then."

"I have to kiss you."

"And I have to groan when you do."

Both of his hands cupped my face, and he kissed me on the lips. Softly at first and then the kiss became deeper, more demanding.

After Paris

His tongue found mine and entwined just as his hands cupped my buttocks and pulled me onto his very prominent, very huge erection.

I couldn't help but rub myself against it through the material of his trousers. He groaned this time into my mouth as he kissed me still. I could feel his hands pushing up the material of my dress until I was sitting with it all bunched up around my waist. His hands were on my now bare buttocks as he held me in place over his hard cock. I threw my head back in abandonment and a wild thought came into my head. I wouldn't even care if the whole restaurant came in now and watched.

His fingers gripped my hips and then they were pushing aside the scrap of material covering the very core of me. He stroked along my opening and groaned loudly when he found me soaking wet. He tore his lips from mine. "You are so fucking wet Alyssa." His voice was deep and husky and made my insides melt.

"I have been all night," I whispered back against his lips. "That's what you do to me Mr. Montgomery."

We stared at each other as his fingers probed some more and then slipped inside me. I moaned as he stroked my clit with his thumb as he moved his fingers inside me. I writhed uncontrollably against his hand as I massaged his huge cock through his trousers. This was exquisite torture. His fingers were working their magic, and I could feel myself beginning to lose control. After all the foreplay had been going on for over a week and I had reached my limit.

"Come for me Alyssa," he whispered in my ear. "Come for me, all over my fingers."

Oh God, this man and his dirty talk was going to be the end of me. But it was those exact words that tipped me over the edge, and I pushed my face into his shoulder to muffle my moaning as I finally let go clamping around his fingers. He held me close as I came back down to earth. What the hell just happened? I had an orgasm in a three Michelin star restaurant with Xavier Montgomery and we hadn't even taken our clothes off.

"Well, that blew your shitty ex's theory out of the window," Xavier breathed against my hair.

"What?" I asked raising my head to look at him. He looked pretty

pleased with himself with a sexy smirk on his face.
"Definitely not frigid," he kissed me softly on the lips. "The exact opposite actually."
I found myself blushing and he laughed.
"You are adorable Miss James."
There was a knock at the door, and I stood up abruptly pulling my dress down over my hips. It was the waiters with the coffee. I needed to go and clean up.
"Just going to the bathroom," I said to Xavier grabbing my bag. He nodded and I followed the waiters out and one of them kindly showed me where the ladies' room was. I looked at myself in the mirror. I looked like a woman who had just had an orgasm. My eyes were dark and dilated and I knew that I needed him in all senses of the word. I cleaned myself quickly and went back to him. He was looking at a message on his phone but put it on the table as soon as I entered the room.
"Shall we go?" I asked.
"You don't want coffee?"
"No. I want you."
His eyes widened and he stood up. "Let's go then."
He strode over to me and took my hand.

CHAPTER TWELVE

Xavier

I don't even remember the drive back in the car. I wanted her so much and all I could hear was her soft moans as I touched her when we were in the restaurant. She was as sexy as fuck, and I actually thought I was going to combust if I didn't have her. The fact she had said so confidently that she wanted me, drove me to distraction.

As soon as we closed the door of the suite behind us, I pushed her up against the wall. My mouth crushed on hers as I pushed myself against her soft curves. Her fingers went to my jacket, she pushed it from my shoulders, and it fell to the floor. She pulled my mouth back to hers and our kiss deepened. Her fingers went to my shirt buttons, and she began to undo them. Shit, she was taking too long. I ripped the shirt undone for her and buttons popped onto the floor, closely followed by my shirt. Her hands travelled over my skin, and I felt like I was on fire. She unzipped my trousers and I felt her take my cock in her hand. I groaned loudly as she stroked me with those long-manicured fingertips. I needed to be inside her. I pulled off my trousers stepping out of my loafers as I did so, and then yanked down my boxers. She stared into my eyes, as she unzipped her dress and then shimmied it down her body kicking it away with her sexy heels. Her underwear was sexy and minimal, pieces of delicate black lace that just covered what it had to. She had hold up stockings on and just the sight of her lightly tanned thighs at the top had me moaning as I pulled her to me. She fell back onto the bed, and I fell on top of her.

"I want you naked," I whispered.

She reached behind her and popped open her bra. Her breasts were magnificent. Full and round and topped with hard pink nipples. I sucked one into my mouth and she let out one of her sexy little moans. I looked at her face and her eyes were closed as I suckled and nipped and caressed those perfect breasts of hers. Her back arched and her hips rose towards mine and I knew I could not hold out for much longer. I needed to be inside her and now. I pulled her panties down her legs and then rolled off her stockings. Fuck, she was perfect. And I had her just where I had always wanted her. I reached over the drawer in the nightstand where I had optimistically stashed a box of condoms earlier when we had arrived and retrieved one. Ripping it open with my teeth I rolled it on my cock. I was so ready.

"Xavier," she whispered. "I need to tell you something…"

"What?" I asked caging her head with my hands as I manoeuvred myself between her legs. I nudged the tip of my cock against her opening, and she moaned. "What do you need to tell me Alyssa?" I pushed a bit more and she moaned again. "Alyssa, can it wait? I really need to fuck you right now."

With a soft cry, she nodded, and I thrust my hips entering her fully. Oh God she felt like velvet around my hard aching cock. I needed to fuck her hard, I couldn't hold back. I began to pump into her slowly at first and then harder and faster. Her legs wrapped themselves around my waist giving me even more access to her. This was so good. It reminded me of that night in the club and the girl with the tattoo, so much like her. Alyssa even smelt like her, the same lemony fragrance in her hair, the same light florally perfume. Fuck I was getting a touch of déjà vu. I looked down at Alyssa writhing beneath me matching each one of my thrusts with one of her own and suddenly I stopped. Alyssa's eyes flew open, and she looked up at me.

"What's wrong?" she asked, her breathing deep and ragged much like my own.

"I know this a shitty thing to say, but you remind me so much of someone…someone I met here in Paris, funnily enough on the same day I met you. I was only attracted to her because she reminded me of you and now you remind me of her, but she had a tattoo on her left shoulder. A blue butterfly…" I trailed off because as I stared down at her, her eyes filled with tears, and she bit her lip. Instinctively I pulled her left shoulder towards me and there it was…the blue butterfly.

I pulled out of her and sat back on my haunches.

"What the fuck?"

"Xavier…" she said tearfully, reaching out to me.

I backed away from her. "Seriously? Alyssa what the fuck is going on here? You fucking worked in a sex club?"

She shook her head. "No. No. I told you on the night that I didn't work there, it was for one night only."

I shook my head not understanding. "But you still were there. In a sex club. Watching people having sex and then you let me fuck you. What the hell?"

I jumped off the bed and pulled the condom off my still annoyingly hard dick and threw it on the floor.

"I was there for research. I told you that too. I said I couldn't come to dinner with you because I had work to do."

"In a fucking sex club?"

"Yes. My editor knew the owner's wife and they let me observe for one night. It was for my story. My book."

"But you didn't just observe, did you?" I shouted at her. "You joined in. You let me fuck you, would you have let anyone fuck you that night Alyssa? For your story?"

She knelt up on the bed and I tried to ignore her naked curves as she looked at me, her eyes imploring me to listen to her.

"No! I knew it was you. I saw you when you came in. I tried to avoid you but then you saw me, and I knew there was no going back. I decided to throw caution to the wind and when I saw the blonde woman approach you, I thought you would go with her. But you didn't and I took my chance."

I walked around the bed looking for my boxers. Fuck. I couldn't have an argument with my hard dick on show.

"Why the fuck would you do that?" I asked as I pulled on my underwear.

"Because I wanted to do something totally out of the ordinary. I wanted to boost the confidence that had been zapped out of me by what happened with Theo, and I had felt the connection with you earlier…because I wanted you."

I stared at her, and I knew what she was saying was true but still it rankled. "So why did you not tell me before now?"

"How do you drop something like that into a conversation? Oh, by the way Xavier, I am the masked girl you fucked in a sex club in Paris."

I ran a frustrated hand through my hair. "Ok. So maybe not like that."

"Then how? I tried to tell you tonight. I couldn't find the words. I was worried about your reaction. I didn't want to ruin things."

I snorted. "Yeah, well they are well and truly fucked now."

I pulled my trousers back on angrily and picked up my shirt with the buttons ripped and shoved my arms in it.

"What are you doing?" she asked, her voice quavering with tears.

"I need to get some fresh air. I need to think about this."

"Please don't leave."

"Don't beg me Alyssa," I said coldly. "I can't bear it when a woman begs me."

I picked up my jacket and checked my phone and wallet were in the pocket as I pulled it on and then without a backward glance, I left the room.

I stopped at the bar downstairs for a JD and coke and drank three before I finally went out to get some night air. I walked aimlessly for ages, just thinking it all over and over in my head. She was right of course. It would have been hard for her to just tell me something like that. And she had tried her hardest to resist me at every turn and originally, she hadn't even wanted to do the story on me. She had been avoiding me for a reason, and that reason I had found out tonight. On the plus side I had finally found Papillon who turned out to be Alyssa, the woman in the mask who I had searched for without finding her. Surely that was a win/win situation? And yet it still bothered me that she didn't tell you up."

I put her down on my bed and pulled the duvet over her. "I am just going to have a quick shower and I will be back."

She nodded and closed her eyes. I showered quickly. I wanted to get back to her and hold her close and let her know I was sorry but when I went into the bedroom, she was sound asleep and so I pulled on some clean boxers and slid in beside her, wrapping my arms around her, hugging her against my chest. Not how I had planned to get her into my bed but at least she was here. We would talk in the morning when hopefully we could sort out this shit. I fell asleep with the smell of lemons from her hair comforting me.

I woke to the sound of the shower in the background. I sat up and my head whirled a bit. JD and wine mix from last night not good. The space beside me was empty and cold. So, she was still angry at me. I stretched up my arms and swung my legs over the side of the bed. Time to eat humble pie for breakfast.

I padded through to the bathroom and watched her through the glass shower door. She was beautiful and perfect. Her body was curvy and womanly and despite how I knew she was feeling about me this morning, my dick did not. Yeah, he never let me down. Under normal circumstances I would have no hesitation in jumping in the shower with her but today…today was different. I watched as she turned off the water and turned to get out and it was then she saw me, her startled eyes meeting mine. I reached for a big fluffy white towel and held it open for her. She walked towards me, and I couldn't help but allow my eyes to leave her face and glide over her body. She took the towel from my hands and wrapped it around her, spoiling my view.

"Morning," I smiled.

"Morning," her voice was soft and devoid of emotion.

"Are you hungry? Thought I would order us some room service."

"Yes. That would be nice."

"What would you like?"

She shrugged. "Normal breakfast stuff." She went to brush past me, but I grabbed her wrist.

After Paris

me sooner. I looked at my watch as I sat on a bench along the river Seine. I had no idea how long I had been sitting there but it had started to get light. It was five in the morning. Tiredness overtook me and I hailed a passing cab to take me back to the hotel.

I crept into the room. Alyssa wasn't in my bed. I guessed she had gone to her own. I wanted to make sure she was ok. I had concluded, as I had sat on that bench, that I was a serious dick head and had treated her badly. She hadn't deserved it. She had done something a bit reckless and wild, which was the way I always lived my life, and I had berated her for it. She hadn't lied to me but instead had just found it hard to tell me the truth. It was a pretty unusual situation to be fair.

She wasn't in her room either and so I called down to the concierge to see if she had checked out. They said not. Ok, so I was a bit worried now. I racked my brains to see if she had told me about any friends in Paris but couldn't remember any. It was then I saw the doors to the balcony open. I went out and there she was in her robe asleep on one of the loungers. She looked beautiful and I hated myself for how I had just left her like I had. She must be freezing. I bent down and pushed a tendril of her hair back off her face. I cupped her cold cheek with my hand, and she stirred and opened her eyes.

"What are you doing out here?" I asked softly.

"Waiting for you," her voice was all croaky from sleep.

"You're freezing…"

"I'm fine."

"Come to bed," I coaxed.

"I'm ok out here."

She was still pissed at me, and I didn't blame her. Too tired to argue with her and wanting to get in my warm bed, I hooked my arms under her and picked her up.

"What are you doing?" she asked as she wound her arms around my neck.

"Taking you to bed,"

"Why?"

I laughed. "Because you are freezing, and I am going to warm

After Paris

"We need to talk," I said gently.

"You think?" she replied her eyes stoking with defiance. "I wanted to talk last night…"

"Yes, I know. I was a dick head, ok? I admit. I fucked up."

"Yes, you did. What I told you wasn't easy for me…not any of it and you behaved like an idiot."

"A complete fucking idiot and so now we agree, can we talk?"

"Let me get dressed. And then *maybe* we can talk."

I let her go and watched as she walked into her room and shut the door. I shook my head and went to phone room service. The best breakfast that George V could offer was on the cards, I had a feeling that I would need all the help I could get.

CHAPTER THIRTEEN

Alyssa

Sitting across the breakfast table from Xavier, I surveyed all the food before me and had to hide my smile. He must have ordered everything on the menu. It looked like a feast for Henry the Eighth…and his entourage.

"Were you expecting guests?" I asked pouring myself a cup of English breakfast tea.

He raised an amused eyebrow. "Just you. I wasn't sure what you liked and so I ordered everything."

"Apart from it being enough food to feed an army, it looks lovely. You know I won't be able to eat it all right?"

"Just eat what you like," he smiled, his eyes twinkling, and my heart soared. Why the fuck does he have to be so handsome? It is so fucking not fair. I am trying to be annoyed and on my high horse but with every gesture, every smile, every word from him, I can feel my resolve not to talk to him slowly disintegrating.

I helped myself to some scrambled eggs and croissants and ate silently whilst he watched me. I swallowed some very excellent egg and looked at him. "Are you just going to sit there and watch me eat?"

"I like watching you eat. How are the eggs? Good?"

"Michelin star good! You really think this hotel is not going to serve good eggs?"

After Paris

He threw back his head and laughed and despite how I felt about him right now, I loved the sound of his laughter and the way his eyes crinkled at the sides.
"Perhaps I will have some," He reached over and helped himself to the eggs and some salmon and a brioche roll.
"What time are we heading back?" I asked looking down at my food and not at him.
"Are you eager to get away from me?"
I didn't answer, just stared at my food as I felt him staring at me.
"Alyssa, I fucked up. I am sorry, ok? I reacted badly. I was just so fucking blown away by the whole thing. I searched for you both you know…"
I looked up at him. "Both?"
"Yeah, you and the masked woman. I didn't know your last name, but you weren't hard to find. I found out straight away, but I decided not to chase you. You had my number and hadn't called and so I assumed you weren't interested. I certainly did not know anything about the woman in the mask."
"Why were you looking for us?" I shook my head. "I mean me. Why?"
"You said it yourself, the connection. You were not the only person to feel it. The funny thing was I felt it with what I thought were two women on the same day. I was intrigued and wanted to find you both and now I know why that wasn't ever going to happen."
"I didn't do it on purpose you know," I blurted out. "It was pure coincidence that you happened to walk into that club on the one and only night I was there."
He nodded. "Yes, I understand that now. And I want you to understand that I told you the truth that night too. I had never been to that club, or any club like it, before. Not really my scene to be honest but as luck would have it, I happened to walk into Masquerade that night and found you."
"Who did you want to find more afterwards, the masked woman with the tattoo or me?"
He took a sip of his coffee. "You fight dirty Miss James."
I stared at him waiting.
"You really want the answer to that question?" he leant forward.

After Paris

over my skin. He looked up at me with those baby blues of his and undid my jeans, sliding his hands down the back and cupping my now scantily clad backside.
"Shit…" I moaned. "Why are you so good at this…."
He laughed softly. "You know I am a playboy, right?"
I grimaced. "Please don't remind me."
He reached up and lowered my bra cups so that both of my breasts fell out into his awaiting hands. He tweaked the hard jutting nipples with his fingertips as he kissed in between both breasts. My hands went to his head, and I ran my fingers through that thick dark hair. The he reached up his hand and cupped it around my neck pulling my face to his, our lips crushed together. The onslaught was merciless. He was taking no prisoners. He stood up and pulled me with him as he clasped his hands under my buttocks and lifted me. I clamped my legs around his waist as he carried me into the bedroom, and we fell together onto the bed. He disrobed and removed his boxers in double quick time. He removed all my clothes even quicker if that was even possible and there, we were naked again. He leant over to the nightstand to get a condom. I sat up and held his arm.
"Not so fast lover boy. My turn…"
I pushed him onto his back, and he watched me as I manoeuvred myself between his legs. I leant down and licked the tip of his penis. He jolted and cursed at the same time. I smiled. I licked the whole length of him this time, just using my tongue and he moaned loudly. Then I took him in my mouth and sucked him, not all of him as he was so big, but three quarters using my hand at the base to slide up and down in rhythm with my mouth.
He jerked beneath me, his hips thrusting up as my mouth took him in.
"Ah fuck…." He moaned as I pushed my mouth and lips just a bit further down his thick shaft, making sure to suck him all the way back up to the tip. I licked my lips and kissed up his body, across his abs, licking his nipples, his hard muscular chest, and his neck. Finally, I reached his lips and kissed them softly. He stared up at me through half closed lust filled eyes.
"Don't even want to know how you are so good at that," he said huskily "If I didn't want to be inside you so much, I'd just let you

carry right on."

"Next time," I smiled seductively as he reached up and pulled me down for a kiss. Our lips were still together as he pushed me onto my back and moved his body over mine. I ran my fingertips across his shoulders and down to his tight, smooth, muscular buttocks and the thought of 'how did I get so lucky' ran through my mind as he tore his lips from mine and reached his hand between my legs and moaned when his fingertips found how wet I was.

"Alyssa, you are so fucking sexy," Xavier said as he leant over to get a condom. He made light work of sliding it onto his cock and positioning himself between my legs again and then he teased me a bit nudging against my slick opening as I pushed my hips towards him.

"Tell me..." he whispered urgently. "Tell me what you want...what you need..."

"You...inside me...now...please..."

"Alyssa...." My name on his lips is like a caress as he slid into me with a groan. He remained still for a moment, and I looked up at him. "You feel like heaven."

My mouth curved into a naughty smile. "Fuck me, Xavier."

"That would be my pleasure..." his voice trailed off as he began to move inside me. Then he began to pump into me, softly at first and then gradually getting harder. He pulled my legs up and placed his hands behind my knees holding them there so that he could thrust into me even deeper. All I could hear were our mutual groans and the soft slapping of our skin as he slammed into me. I looked up at him and he looked like a male model, his hair falling across his forehead, his eyes closed as he lost himself in the moment, his strong arms holding my legs apart. I loved the way that his whole body is totally attuned with mine, every touch, every movement...just everything. A feeling washed over me, and I know I couldn't ignore it. I am in love with Xavier Montgomery, and it has all been leading to this. This is the real thing and instantly I know that everything I have ever felt for any man in the past has been nothing.... nothing compared to this. When I looked up into his face his eyes are open, and he is looking straight into my eyes. I closed mine afraid that he will

After Paris

see, see how I feel. For some reason I know that it is too early to admit my true feelings for him. He is not ready yet and he has not opened himself to me entirely, only telling me what he thinks I want to hear. He pushed in deeper, and I felt myself losing control. I am so close to letting go and I can tell by his eyes that he knows. He thrust his hips again and it finally pushed me over the edge. I screamed out his name as I pulsed around his cock, and he groaned loudly as he thrust a few more times and then threw back his head as his hips jerked as he came hard.

He fell onto me, his breathing deep and erratic. His head was buried in my neck as I held him, my arms wrapped around his neck. He was still inside me, and I liked it.

"You are beyond incredible," he whispered in my ear.

"You're not bad yourself," I smiled, and he lifted his head to look at me, his eyebrows raised.

"Not bad?" He asked letting out a short sharp laugh.

"Hmmmh...for a playboy."

"Why don't we stay?"

"Stay?"

"Here...in this hotel for the whole weekend."

I am silent for a few seconds. I can't believe he wants to be with me the whole weekend.

"Really?" I asked. "Can we?"

"Alyssa, we can do whatever we want to do. I just need to make a few phone calls and we are set. You ok to stay?"

I nodded trying to curb my happiness and enthusiasm at the thought of staying with him the whole weekend.

He grinned. "Think carefully before you answer. Will you be able to put up with my endless demands for your body?"

I pretended to think about it for a minute. "Em, yes I think I would be kind of ok with that..."

He bent his head to kiss my lips softly. "Oh really?" he said against my lips. "Well let's stay then but right now I need to go to the bathroom. Don't you go anywhere ok?"

He pulled out of me, and I gave a little moan.

"Just so you know," he said over his shoulder as he walked to the bathroom and I admired the back view of his naked body, those broad shoulders tapering down into slim hips and peachy round buttocks. "Those little moans you make when we are fucking drive me into the stratosphere."

I lay back amongst the pillows and giggled to myself. I could think of worse things to do than having sex with Xavier Montgomery all weekend in the George V hotel in Paris. Someone please pinch me.

CHAPTER FOURTEEN

Xavier

I disposed of the used condom in the bin and then looked at myself in the mirror. Did I, Xavier Montgomery, just ask a woman to spend the whole weekend with me? Unheard of. I had never done that before. And yet as soon as the words were out of my mouth and I saw the light shine in her eyes, I knew that I had done the right thing. I was even looking forward to spending time with her. She was everything I liked in bed, demure and yet so fucking sexy. When she had taken me in her mouth, I had almost lost it. And that body...that curvaceous, warm, soft body was just made for me to worship and to adore and to fuck to the moon and back again. But more than all of that, I liked her. I liked being with her and I had never felt more in sync woman before. I had always loved women in a sexual way but never liked them, never wanted to spend my free time with them. I remember that I had once made the mistake of inviting one of the women I was bedding to accompany me to an event and then she had turned psycho on me. Being clingy, ringing me night and day, annoying the hell out of me, and thinking she was my girlfriend. I never did it again.

I washed my dick in the basin, it was still semi hard just thinking about Alyssa and her sweet little moans and groans as I had pummelled into her. I could fuck her all day and all night long and never get tired of her. The thought of her being with that dick head Constantine made me sick to my stomach and the way he had treated her made me see red. I seriously regretted not punching his lights out when we were at school, at least I would have felt vindicated now. How could he have ever made her feel like she was frigid? Or even mentioned words like that to her? The woman in my bed was the total opposite of anything like that. Sounded like he was blaming her for his own short comings…and he obviously had a tiny little dick. I smiled at myself in the mirror. As if an idiot like that could satisfy a woman like Alyssa. It still fucking annoyed me though, thinking that he ever had his slimy hands on her.

I went back in the bedroom and Alyssa was sitting up against the headboard with the duvet wrapped around her. She looked beautiful. I saw her eyes roam over my nakedness, and I smiled. I slid into the bed next to her and pulled her warm body into my arms.
"You were ages," she said. "What were you doing in there?"
"Thinking about you and that dickhead," the words were out of my mouth before I could stop myself. I felt her stiffen beside me. "I going to be completely honest here Alyssa, it really riles me that he ever had his hands on you."
"Please don't…" She pulled away from me and sat up hugging her knees. "Not good memories for me. If it is of any consolation, I regret ever getting involved with him."
"At least put me out of my misery and tell me he was shit in bed…"
"Xavier!"
I sat up next to her. "He was shit, wasn't he?"
"Stop it. I don't want to talk about him."
"Did you love him?"
Her head turned sharply to look at me. "No. I was never in love with him."
She said it so vehemently, so I felt some satisfaction from her answer.
"For your information, I have never been jealous, not of anyone, and I don't like the feeling…thinking of you and him makes me so mad."

After Paris

She wound her arm through mine and laid her head on my shoulder "There is no need to be jealous of him…he was just a small piece of *merde*."

I laughed at her use of French. "Is that the only French you know?"

She straightened her back and had the gall to look offended. "No…I know other words too."

"Such as?"

"*Petit Dejeuner, café au lait,*" she tilted her head to one side and pretended to think. "Yep, that's it. That's all I've got."

I laughed. Fuck, she was so cute, and she had got me off the subject of her ex again. She was good at that, steering me away from a bad mood.

"Want me to speak dirty to you in French?" I asked.

She closed her eyes and a sexy grin spread across her lips. "You could say anything to me in French and it would sound like sex."

I pursed my lips trying not to smile. "Oh really? So, you were telling the truth when you said it turned you on?"

"Of course, especially when those French words come out of *your* mouth."

I lay back down and pulled her on top of me. Her soft curves pressed against my body and of course she could feel how hard I was.

"Wow, you are hard again," she breathed as she ran her fingertips down my cock.

"Is that a problem?"

She shook her head. "No problem at all."

"Good because I think it's going to be hard a lot over these next couple of days."

She sat up and straddled my waist. Her beautiful breasts beckoned, and I reached up and cupped them both in my hands. "Do you not think they are too big?" she asked her eyes dark with lust.

"Most definitely not. They are perfect," I tweaked her nipples between my thumb and finger, and they hardened and puckered beneath my touch.

"They are just about the best pair of breasts I have ever seen. I could look at them all day."

She bent towards me, so they are now right near my lips.

"Praise indeed. How about if you put them between those luscious lips of yours instead?"

"I can do that," my voice had gone all husky again. It seems to do that a lot when I am near her. I opened my lips and took one of her nipples in my mouth. I suckled and nipped with my mouth and my tongue and my teeth whilst looking up at her as she threw her head back emitting those tiny soft groans which drove me to distraction. To take me even further over the edge, she was rubbing her pussy over my cock very time she moved. She sat up and I took that moment to reach and grab a condom from the side. I ripped it open quickly and rolled it on as she watched me with heavily lidded eyes. I guided her with my hands on her hips and glided slickly inside her, all of me right up to the hilt. I groaned loudly because it felt so good, her pussy wet and tight around me. She began to move her hips and I reached up and took those beautiful breasts in my hands, whilst thrusting my hips up to meet hers. As she moved her hips back and forth, her boobs bounced tantalisingly, and I rotated my hips grinding inside of her as a thousand stars went off behind my eyes. She was riding me like a porn star, and I was once again blown away by the difference between the shy blushing Alyssa and this total sex goddess riding my cock like it was as natural to her as breathing. I had to fuck her hard.

"I need to fuck you from behind" I almost growled.

Her eyes flew open, and she smiled sexily. She hopped off me with a small moan and I moved behind her pulling her hips up into the air with my hands and pushing her legs apart. The sight alone was enough but with a hard thrust of my hips I pushed into her, and I swear this time I actually saw stars in front of my eyes. At this angle I could push deeper than ever, and she moaned her appreciation. I was obviously hitting the right spot.

"Xavier...." she moaned. "Oh God.... Xavier...."

Hearing her voice saying my name in throes of passion made me want more of her and so I pounded just that bit harder.

"Oh...Xavier I'm coming...oh..." She threw her head back and her pussy pulsed around me, and I could feel myself losing control. This was too much. I had had some hot sex in the past,

After Paris

but this was on another level. I thrust inside her a few more times and jumped over the edge with her, coming hard and loud.

We spent the whole day fucking. We showered together and I fucked her against the shower wall as the water cascaded over our bodies. I had her on the dining table after we had finished the food we ordered from room service; her legs spread wide as I pounded into her. I fucked her from behind out on the balcony as the sun began to set in the Parisian sky. I couldn't get enough of her. She was addictive. It was like we were in our own little bubble, ensconced in our suite in George V and nothing and nobody existed outside of that. I hadn't ever spent this much time with anyone in like forever and yet I wasn't bored. In fact, the more I got to know her to more I wanted to know. Usually, I didn't even ask the woman I had just fucked her last name, but Alyssa was like a drug. I had told her things I have never told anyone, not even Gabe and Ed, and that made her a dangerous drug. She had a way of making me open like a flower in full bloom. I knew some of it was just how she was and her journalist line of questioning and getting information out of people, but I think now she was just interested in getting to know me for her own benefit. She hadn't got her notebook or recorder out once the whole time we were together and knew that we had now transcended into something entirely separate. The time had come to tell her the truth…to tell her about Guillaume…

Lying in bed that night after just fucking each other senseless once again, I held her in my arms, her head on my chest and me stroking her hair and loving the feel of her body close to mine. Our legs were entwined, and we were both in that post coital state of mind…relaxed, sated, and happy. I took a deep breath. "Alyssa," I began slowly. "I want to tell you about my father…" I felt her body tense slightly, but her voice was calm and normal when she answered.
"Ok, only if you want to."
"I do."
"I'm listening."
"To explain my relationship with my father I have to start the

summer I turned thirteen and Guillaume had just turned seven...."

"Guillaume?"

"My brother."

There was short silence. "I didn't know you had a brother."

I took another deep breath. "I haven't now...I had a brother once."

I could tell she wanted to lift her head and look at me, needed to look at me, but she kept still perhaps sensing that I was more likely to talk if she wasn't looking at me. Sometimes it was easier that way, when you didn't have to look at someone as you explained or talked about something that was difficult.

"Tell me," she said gently.

"His name was Guillaume. He was six years younger than me. He was a beautiful little boy. Blonde, blue eyed, sweet natured and happy. I in contrast was at that awkward age, thinking I knew everything when in fact I knew nothing. I was wild and wayward, and I hated authority. I got into all kinds of trouble and scrapes and my parents were always being called into school about me, something I had done or not done. I can't even remember how many times I got threatened with suspension or expulsion, but somehow my parents always smoothed it over. The amount of money they had to give the school, just so I could stay, would have probably rebuilt the school ten times over. Guillaume idolised me. I was his big brother, bold and fearless, I couldn't do anything wrong in his seven-year-old eyes. That summer was spent in Hampshire at my family estate. It was a warm summer, strange for England I know, but it was for once a summer like no other. The days were long and filled with sunshine and picnics and lazing about doing nothing. I, of course, was bored out of my head. I wanted to go swim in the lake we had on our estate. It was forbidden by my father. The water was deep and there were pockets that were dangerous. He forbade me to go, even though I was a good swimmer. I excelled at sports on school. I was good at most of them, I don't know if you noted I have a competitive streak in me?"

I felt her smile on my skin.

"Anyway, I decided I was going. No one could stop me. I put on

After Paris

my swim shorts under my trousers and ran down to the lake. Guillaume followed me. I told him that he was not to come into the water but to stand on the bank and wait for me. I waded out and the water was wonderfully cool on a hot day. I called back to him telling him, no boasting, how good it was. I swam out to the little island in the middle of the lake and got out of the water. I turned to wave to Guillaume, but he wasn't there, not where I had left him. Then I saw him, his little blonde head bobbing in the water. I remember feeling panic as Guillaume was not a good swimmer. I had promised to teach him but of course, I had never made the time. I shouted at him to go back but he couldn't hear me. I remember feeling annoyed because he hadn't listened to me and jumped back into the water. As I swam, I could see he was struggling. He kept going under and calling my name as he came up for air. I swam as hard and fast as I could to reach him but when I reached where I had last saw him, he wasn't there. I dove under the water, but it was hard to see. The water was murky and filled with reeds and other plants. I couldn't see him. I went down and came up again for air at least four times before I saw him. He was still with his eyes closed and I knew I had to get him out as soon as possible. His legs were entwined with weeds and plants, and I had to rip them from him before I could pull him up to the surface and swim back with him to the shore. I didn't know what to do. I stood there just looking at him lying there before I started shouting and screaming and thank God the gardener and our housekeeper had heard my shouts and came running. The gardener began CPR and tried to revive him, he tried over and over and by this time my mother and father had been told and come running down. My mother was screaming, and my father pushed the gardener back and did mouth to mouth, but Guillaume just lie there...." I trailed off as I remembered and swallowed hard. My mouth had gone dry. I couldn't say the actual words. I could feel Alyssa's tears on my chest.

"My father blamed me and my stupid reckless behaviour. My mother went into some kind of breakdown. She began drinking a lot and taking pills. One day she took an overdose saying that she wanted to die but luckily my father found her and took her to hospital. Our perfect summer had turned into a nightmare. My father couldn't bear to look at me and wouldn't even allow me to attend my own brother's funeral. That's when he decided to pack me off to boarding school. To be honest I was glad to go. All that was left in that house was sadness. The walls screamed with it, and I wanted to be alone with my grief."

Alyssa raised her head. Her face wet from tears.

"You know it was an accident, right? That it wasn't your fault?" Her voice was filled with yet more unshed tears.

"But it was. I should have looked after him. I should have listened."

"But you were only a child yourself…only thirteen."

"But old enough to know better. The year afterwards my mother and father split up and eventually got a divorce. From then on, I spent the summers with my mother in France. My father never asked to see me. He paid for my school and anything I needed materially but I never went back to Hampshire. I saw him once a few years back at an event…he treated me like a stranger. It hurt…it hurt me badly."

"Oh God, Xavier," Alyssa started crying again, huge tears that fell down her cheeks silently and onto my chest.

I hugged her to me. Her tears moved me, but I had cried enough in the past and had no more tears left in me. My tears now were silent and visible to no one else but me.

"You are the only person who now knows the whole story. Gabe and Ed know that I had a brother who died but they have never asked me, and I have never offered the whole story. They were good friends when I was thirteen and they are still always there for me now. I like to think that Guillaume sent them to me in his place."

She nodded as she wiped the tears from her cheeks. "I agree. You can see that they care about you like brothers would."

"I feel exhausted," I murmured, and I did, I felt like I could sleep for a year."

"Let's sleep," Alyssa said softly.

I closed my eyes and felt a kind of serenity coming over me and I drifted off.

Sometime during the night, I awoke. I was spooning Alyssa and

After Paris

had my arm around her waist. I was hard and wanted her again. I reached up and cupped her breasts and she stirred, moaning sleepily, her eyes still closed. I kissed her neck and she moaned again softly. I reached down and ran a fingertip along her sex. She was wet. I groaned and trailed kisses along her neck.

"Xavier," she whispered and turned to me. Our lips met softly at first and then our kiss became deeper, hungry, and demanding. I grabbed a condom and rolled it on quickly and then entered her with one hot thrust of my hips as she groaned against my lips. As I moved inside her I knew. This was different, this wasn't fucking anymore. I looked down at her face, but her eyes were closed, and I wondered if she felt it too. I watched her and when she opened her eyes, she stared up at me with silent questions, questions that I was not prepared for and couldn't answer right in that moment.

I was making love to a woman for the first time ever and for some reason I could not explain, it scared the life out of me.

CHAPTER FIFTEEN

London

Alyssa

I put the last of my clothes in my overnight case and closed it. The car was coming any minute to take us to the airport for our flight home, back to London.
Xavier had been quiet and distant this morning at breakfast and afterwards and I knew it was because he was trying to find the words to tell me that this, whatever it was, was over and it was all back to him being a playboy businessman and me being a journalist and going our separate ways. I was trying to be grown up and civilised about everything, but I admit I was struggling. I had just spent two days and nights in his bed and it had been everything I had thought it would be and more, but like an idiot I hadn't thought beyond that...hadn't wanted to because I knew he didn't do relationships and that it was all about sex...and he had had me now, in fact he had had me lots of times, in every way possible. If this morning was anything to go by, his interest in me was already waning. I had to man up over this. I had to pretend that it didn't matter to me, that it was all I ever wanted too.

He came into the bedroom and smiled. "Ready to go? The car is downstairs waiting for us."
I forced a smile to my lips. "Yep, All ready."
"Let's go then."
I nodded and followed him with my case and my handbag.

After Paris

The ride to the airport was strained. It was like we had nothing else to say to each other. It was awful. I felt sick all the way there. On the plane he apologised, saying that he had to catch up on some work and kept his attention on his laptop until, ashamed and heartbroken, I fell asleep. I woke up just as we were circling over London City Airport and just had time to refresh myself before we landed. He held my hand in the car to my house but didn't really talk to me, looking at his mobile and generally ignoring me and I was kind of relieved when we finally pulled up outside my house. Holy shit, now I had to listen to him telling me he didn't want to see me anymore now that we were back home.

"So, home again," he smiled as the car came to a complete stop and the driver got out to get my luggage.

"Yes, home again."

Fuck I sounded like a parrot. Get in first Alyssa. Show him that you don't care.

"Well thank you so much for a lovely time. It was great." I went to get out of the car, but he leant over me and pulled the door shut again.

"Alyssa…"

"Xavier?"

He let out a huge breath. "I em…I need some time this week to catch up on work, but I will call you."

"I am so busy this week myself. I have all I need for the interview and need to write it up and then must get back to my novel, so completely get where you are coming from."

He raised an eyebrow. "So, you understand then?"

"Of course," I replied brightly. "I understand perfectly. No commitments. No ties. No big deal."

He frowned. "Not exactly what I meant but…"

Oh God. Please don't say anymore…I get it…. I get it….

"Thanks once again. Harriet will be in touch with you about when the interview will be in the magazine. They'll probably call you to do a photo shoot."

"Alyssa?"

Something about how he said my name made me turn and look at him. Look into his mediterranean sea blue eyes. He looked so

handsome and so beautiful I just had to do it. I leant in and kissed his lips. The kiss was soft and sweet. He kissed me back, which kind of made this even harder and so I pulled away reluctantly.
"Goodbye Xavier."
I got out of the car, but he followed me right up to my door.
"I'll call you," he said again awkwardly looking down at his feet.
No, you won't. We both know that you won't.
I nodded but didn't answer. I watched as he walked back to the car and as he got in, he turned to look at me. I gave him a tiny wave and he smiled. I watched the car pull away and then went indoors and sobbed my heart out.

"What the fuck?" Naomi almost shouted angrily.
"I know, I know. It's my fault. I let my guard down and trusted him. I should never have done that."
I had dropped by to see Naomi and finally take the dress back that she had lent me. It had been seven days since we had been back from Paris and just like I had suspected, Xavier had not called me. Not one peep. To say I was hurt was nowhere near the truth of how I felt. I felt like a piece of *merde*.
Naomi poured the fresh coffee she had just made into glass coffee cups. "You did what any normal person would do. He is not normal."
Despite how Xavier had treated me and hadn't called me for a whole week, I still felt the need to defend him. He had revealed his innermost secrets to me and perhaps he was regretting it, telling me so much, afraid that I would write about everything in my story on him. I hadn't of course. I would never tell anyone what he had told me. Instead, I had been honest and fair and had tried to put my own personal emotions and feelings aside. I think I had done a pretty damn good piece of work. Harriet had loved it. There was hardly any editing, and she was happy to run the story almost as I had written it, which was unheard of for Harriet. I was both elated and devastated at the same time.
I sighed. "It's complicated Naomi…"
"So, you need to feel like a worthless piece of shit because things are complicated? I hope he is feeling like a shit too, because that's what he is," she sipped her coffee. "I would love to give him a

After Paris

piece of my mind."
Despite how I felt I couldn't help smiling. Naomi was such a good friend, but she really didn't understand the half of it. She wouldn't be able to understand the intensity of my feelings for Xavier and that inexplicable bond that had been between us. Right now, all she could see was her friend hurt and angry and desolate.

"You make excellent coffee by the way," I smiled sipping the delicious beverage.

She eyed me over the rim of her coffee cup. "That's it Alyssa. Change the subject like you always do when things get a bit painful. That has always been your coping mechanism since I have known you. Sometimes you just need to confront things head on you know."

I nodded. "And I will. I just need time to process stuff in my head. Right now, I am in limbo land. I have no idea how he feels about me. He hasn't said he doesn't want to see me but then has made no moves towards me either."

"So why don't *you* call him?"

I was shaking my head before the words were even out of her mouth. "No. Definitely not."

"What?" She laughed. "I thought you were an independent, twenty first century woman. Seriously why are you waiting for him to call you?"

"Because…because he just needs to. I do not chase men."

Naomi put her coffee cup down and made direct eye contact with me. "But he is not men, he's Xavier Montgomery."

I stared back at her. She was right of course. There was no reason why I should not call him. I had a certain amount of pride, but I could push that aside for him…only for him.

I nodded. "I'll call him later. I need to pop into to see Harriet and then I'll call him." I saw her wide-eyed disbelieving look. "I promise, ok?"

I walked down the Embankment to the offices of *Aristocrat* magazine with a slight spring in my step. I had talked myself in and out of calling him a hundred times since speaking to Naomi, but now I had decided I was definitely going to call him. It made me feel lighter, like a weight had been taken off my shoulders.

However he received my call would give me the definitive answer. He either wanted me or he didn't. I would know from this call. I wasn't stupid. I could always read between the lines.
I knocked on Harriet's door and her gruff voice called out for me to enter. When she saw it was me, she beamed a smile.
"If it is not my star reporter. How are you, Alyssa?" She gestured for me to sit in the comfy chair opposite her and I did, crossing my legs. "The Montgomery piece was excellent, but you know that of course. We are trying to set up a shoot with him over the next few days and hopefully we will run your story in the next issue. He loved it by the way."
I stared at her, my stomach lurching. "He's seen it already?"
She looked at me for a long moment. "Of course. I sent a copy to him straight away. He asked me to. Is that a problem?"
I swallowed hard and shook my head. *He's seen my story and not even called me.*
"No...no of course not. I'm happy he liked it."
Harriet leant back in her chair and studied me her gaze unwavering. "You slept with him, didn't you?"
I tried to avoid her eyes, but she was good, and she saw the answer before I even said anything.
"Don't worry, it didn't come out in your writing. You are much too professional for that. I am just well trained in the art of reading people. Did it happen after you started writing the story or in Paris when you met him the first time?"
I let out a long breath. "In Paris. Before the story."
She nodded. "Guessed that. And how is it now between you both? I take it there are some issues?"
I tilted my head to one side. "Let's just say it is unfinished."
She raised her eyebrows. "Not like you Alyssa, leaving business unfinished."
I shrugged. "Guess there is always a first time."
"Nonsense. Whatever it is between you both needs to be resolved. Does he know you are in love with him?"
My eyes flicked up to hers. *Fuck she was good.*
"No and I intend to keep it that way."
"Alyssa. As much as it pains me to say this, sometimes you need to make it clear to someone how you are feeling, to men

After Paris

especially. They are notoriously slow and a bit dense on picking up on these things."
I shook my head. "I am not putting myself out there to be hurt again Harriet. You saw me after Theo."
"I did. But there is one difference here. You didn't love Theo Constantine."
"Which kind of makes it even worse for me doesn't it?"
"Does Montgomery love you?"
I let out a short sharp laugh. "No. It was just sex and the conquest for him. I guess he talked to me a bit more than he had in the past with his other women, but that was only because I was there to do a job."
Harriet stood up and turned her back to me looking out at the view I loved so much. "Don't sell yourself short Alyssa. You are a bright, beautiful young woman and any man would be lucky to have you and if Xavier bloody Montgomery can't see that then he must be a fool."
I smiled sadly. "I think the only fool around here is me."
She turned back to me. "You are no fool Alyssa. Just a woman."

I thought about the conversation with Harriet for the rest of the day. I still hadn't called Xavier and I stared at my mobile now checking my messages for the thousandth time that day. Still nothing. I couldn't believe he had read my story and not called me to comment or tell me how he was feeling about it. It hurt. Not only had he abandoned me personally, but he didn't even have the decency to at least acknowledge me in the professional sense. I felt angry, hurt tears spring to my eyes, and I brushed them away with the back of my hand as soon as they appeared. Perhaps I had read him all wrong. Perhaps he really was just a playboy womaniser with no backbone and a superficial lifestyle but even as I thought it, I knew that it wasn't true. I had seen him, the real him, over the time I spent with him, and I knew I was right. And that hurt even more. Because he was kind, feeling, honourable man and yet he was treating me like this. I couldn't call him. I threw my phone on the sofa and went up to have a nice long relaxing bath and a glass of champagne. It wouldn't erase the hurt I felt, I knew that, but at least it would blur it a bit.

CHAPTER SIXTEEN

Xavier

I stared down at my JD and coke and wondered how many I had had. I couldn't remember and I was past caring. I was waiting for Eduardo and Gabe in the bar of the Corinthia Hotel but had arrived early as I hadn't been able to concentrate on my work today and I needed to get out of the office. I was slowly but surely on my way to being out of my head drunk but again I didn't care. Anything to dull the ache I felt inside. Alcohol was my answer, and it was doing a grand old job.

I saw Gabe come into the bar and waved to him. He came over and sat down opposite me, eyeing me with concern.

"Hi mate. How many have you had already?"

I shrugged. "I don't know. Does it matter?"

"Unlike you to get blotto," He called the waitress and ordered a beer for him and one for Eduardo who was on his way.

"And another of these," I added to the waitress waving my drink in the air.

I saw Gabe look at me again.

"What?" I snapped. "So, I can't get drunk when I want to?"

He held up his hands in mock surrender.

"You do whatever you want Xavier. I am not judging."

I tossed the rest of the liquid into my mouth and swallowed it

After Paris

down with relish. "Well good because I don't need to be judged at the moment."

In my peripheral vision I saw Eduardo arrive in the bar. He looked around and saw us and headed over. He sat next to Gabe and stared at me.

"Fuck, someone started the party without us," he said looking at Gabe who raised his eyebrows.

"Don't you start," I said sitting back and looked from Gabe to Eduardo. They were both just looking at me waiting for me to speak. What could I say? I fucked up again. Xavier 'Fuck Up' Montgomery that was me.

The waitress arrived with our drinks, and I grabbed mine like I hadn't had a drink for years and knocked back half of it. I saw my friends look at each other as they tentatively sipped their beer.

"Want to talk about it?" Eduardo asked quietly.

"Nope!"

"Yes, you do," Gabe said. "Let's talk about the elephant in the room. Alyssa James. There I said it."

I glared at him. "I said I am not talking about it."

"Xavier…come on. We're your friends. You need to open up," Eduardo urged me.

"Yes, well that's just it. I opened up a bit too much lately."

"So, you have finally been open and honest with a woman. What's so bad about that?" Eduardo asked leaning back in his chair. "I mean if it was going to be anyone, it would be Alyssa."

"You know she was the woman in the club," I blurted out.

They both stared at me.

"What?" Eduardo looked shocked. "The woman with the butterfly tattoo?"

"Yep. Alyssa James and butterfly woman. One in the same."

Gabe let out a long whistle. "Holy fuck."

"Is that why you're fucked up?" Eduardo asked. "Because she worked in a sex club? Hey there are worse things…"

I shook my head. "No. She didn't work there. It is a long story, but she isn't a sex club hostess."

"Didn't see that one coming," Gabe said taking another swig of his beer. "And she was about to marry that little shit head Constantine. I can't believe that either. That is some kind of shit show."

I snorted a laugh. "Yeah. Can you believe that? That makes me madder than I can even think about."
They looked at each other again.
"So, is this what this is all about?" Eduardo waved his beer bottle towards me. "You are getting out of your head because she had a past relationship with Constantine?"
I shook my head again. "If I am honest, it does bother me. But that is all in her past and there is nothing I can do about that. It is the present I am worried about, and I have fucked up big time with her on that. I said I would call her, and I haven't. Not all week since we have been back from Paris."
Eduardo snorted. "Oh, fuck man. Why not?"
I shrugged. "Because I am a fuck up."
Gabe leant forward. "Define 'fuck up'".
"She knows more about me than I have ever told anyone, even you guys. It scares me. She has found out that the rich playboy that everyone writes about, is just a man, a man with issues and emotional baggage."
"Have you asked her?" Eduardo asked softly. "Asked her how she feels?"
"What good would that do? It won't make it all go away, will it?"
"No. But it may not be such an issue for her. Maybe she is brave enough to take you on just as you are. Just as you can't change her past, you can't change your own either."
I smiled. "You know Eduardo you should be a lawyer or something when you grow up."
Both Eduardo and Gabe grinned and then they both stopped as they looked over my shoulder.
"What?" I said just about to turn when Gabe grabbed my arm.
"Don't look round but Theo Constantine has just walked in with his little entourage."
I turned to look and there he was over by the bar chatting and laughing with some other suits, his plastic too good-looking face laughing like he hadn't a care in the world. Well, he had. Me. I stood up and both Gabe and Eduardo pulled me back down again.
"Not a good idea," Eduardo said shaking his head. "You go over

After Paris

there in your state, and it will just be trouble with a capital T."
"What the fuck is he doing here? We have never bumped into him since we left school, and he walks in the exact bar we are in now?" Gabe looked across at Constantine and his crowd at the bar.
"Maybe he is looking for trouble," I growled. "And here I am." I stood up again and again my friends pulled me back down in my seat.
"You knew he was going to be here, didn't you?" Eduardo was watching me carefully. "How did you find out?"
I grinned. "A little birdie told me."
"Let's just leave. We'll go to another bar," Eduardo suggested.
"No fucking way!" I answered angrily. "I am not scared of him and never will be. We are staying put." I glared over at them just as Constantine looked our way, a look of recognition crossing his smarmy features.
"Oh fuck," Ed said sitting back in his chair "He's coming over."
"Good!" I growled. "I am ready for the arsehole."
"Gentlemen," Theo Constantine greeted us like we were his long-lost friends. "What a small world."
"Yes, isn't it just," I answered.
"Well, well if it isn't Xavier Montgomery being his normal friendly and amicable self. Heard you were setting the financial world on fire. And here you all are like the three Musketeers, just like at school. Montgomery, Espinosa, and Elliot, those who could do no wrong."
"What the fuck is that supposed to mean?" I spat. "Leave while you can."
"I think you should leave Constantine," Eduardo interrupted putting his beer down on the table.
"Yeah, well guess what you are not the Head boy anymore Montgomery, surrounded by your prefects and telling me what to do. But I am leaving, anyway. Can't say it was nice to see you," he went to walk away but then turned back "Oh yes, forgot to mention, How's Alyssa?"
I stood up and batted away both Gabe and Eduardo as they tried to pull me away. I pushed a warning finger almost into his smarmy face. "Don't you even say her name."

Constantine laughed. "There you go again telling me what to do. I suppose you fucked her. You fuck every woman you meet from what I hear. Guess you lucked out with Alyssa. Bit too cold and detached for my taste but I had a good time warming her up for you."

Both Gabe and Eduardo stood up at that and stepped in the middle of us.

"Leave now Constantine," Gabe warned.

"Or what?" he sneered.

We all stared at each other in silence. I was so close, so close to punching him.

"Anyway Montgomery," he said over his shoulder as he finally backed down. "Never liked you much but I thought you could do better than to scrape up my sloppy seconds. Enjoy my leftovers."

Gabe, Eduardo and I all looked at each other and then they gave me a silent nod and I tapped Constantine on the shoulder, as he turned, I smashed my fist into his face. There was an awful cracking sound and then he just fell back onto the floor. He was out cold, blood trailing from his nose. There were gasps all around us and a lot of running about from the staff as the three of us stared at him on the floor.

"Fuck, that hurt!" I moaned lifting my hand which was already beginning to swell across the knuckles.

"To be honest, if you hadn't done that I would have," Eduardo said looking at my hand. He grabbed the ice out of my JD and wrapped it in a napkin and placed it on my hand.

"Aagh" I groaned.

"Ok, so at best we are looking at common assault. Worst he could sue you for actual bodily harm," Eduardo was already on the phone calling an ambulance. "Gabe, take Xavier home. I'll deal with this here."

We looked at Constantine on the floor, who was just coming around and starting to moan.

"I will deal with him. I am your lawyer. Gabe, go… and try and get some black coffee down him."

As we drove away in the Uber waiting outside, courtesy of Gabe's quick thinking, I felt bad leaving Eduardo behind.

After Paris

"Do you think Eduardo will be ok?" I asked wincing at the pain coming from my hand.
"Better than Constantine," Gabe grinned. "Fuck that was a great punch!"
I couldn't help but grin back. "Try telling that to my hand."
"Want to go to A&E?" Gabe asked looking down at my right hand.
"No. Can we go to Alyssa's instead?"
Gabe gave me a sideways glance. "Do you think that's a good idea man? You're off your head and you're injured."
"Yes, I need to see her, and I need to see her now."
"Ok. What's her address? I need to tell the driver."
I typed her name in my phone awkwardly with my left hand and handed it to Gabe. "Here."
Gabe looked down "Pimlico. Oh, how sweet, you have her name and address in your phone."
"Gabe? Fuck off, ok?"
Gabe laughed as he gave the driver the address.

We pulled up outside her house some twenty minutes later. How I wasn't sick in the car I'll never know. Gabe got out first and helped me to the front door. There were lights on, thank God, so that meant at least she was home. Gabe propped me up against the wall and rang her doorbell. The lights in the hallway went on and I heard her sweet voice call out.
"Who is it?"
Gabe grinned at me and made a little heart with his fingers.
"Hi Alyssa. It's me Gabe, Xavier's friend."
The door unlocked and she opened the door hesitantly. She smiled at Gabe and then saw me propped against the wall a wet soggy napkin tied around my hand. Her look changed into one of concern.
"Gabe?" she asked. "What happened?"
"Can we come in and I'll explain," Gabe grabbed me wrapping an arm around my waist.
"Yes of course. Come in." She stood back and Gabe helped me in. As I passed her, I tried to look at her, but she avoided my eyes staring down at the floor.

He wasn't naked. He had boxers on, but I could feel his erection through the material pressing against my buttocks and lower back. Xavier. I feigned sleep whist I thought how best to deal with this. He couldn't treat me like this. He hadn't called or texted for a week but then just thought it was ok to get into bed with me and make me want him again. And I did want him…. I always wanted him.

His hand was gently creeping up under my pyjama top, skimming over my skin leaving a trail of goose bumps in its wake.

I moaned softly and encouraged by this he moved his hand higher just tracing the outline of my breast.

"Oh Robert," I moaned with a smile on my face. "That feels so good!"

The hand halted its ascent, and he sat up. "Who the fuck is Robert?"

I sat up too and studied him in the early morning light. He looked great, his hair dishevelled and his face as angry as hell.

"None of your business and what are you doing in my bed?"

"Who the fuck is Robert Alyssa?"

I jumped out of the bed. "Like I said none of your business. Now please get out of my bed and go back to the sofa."

"I came to talk to you…"

"Yeah?" I folded my arms over my chest, "Well you have a very funny way of talking. It felt like you were trying to seduce me."

"I was waking you up slowly."

"I call bullshit on that. You were initiating sex."

He groaned and lay back amongst the pillows. "Oh, shit Alyssa. Don't say things like that when I have an erection as big as the Shard."

"Is that all you can think about?" I asked and this time I am truly angry. "You come here in the dead of night, drunk, disorderly, injured and I let you in my house, no questions asked. Oh, and this is after you don't call or message me for a week and another thing, did I mention, you did not call me for a week? And then on top of all that, you try and have sex with me."

"Alyssa, please stop saying sex…and can we take the volume down a bit please? My head is still killing me."

My mouth opened in amazement. "Get out of my room, better

still get out of my house."
He smiled that sexy grin of his, the panty melting one that I couldn't resist, and I hated that he was not taking me seriously.
"I mean it Xavier; you need to leave."
"Angry Alyssa," he said throwing back the duvet and walking around the bed to me. "That turns me on."
I try and ignore his perfect body and focus on one thing, the door. If he won't leave I will. I made a move towards it and had my hand on the door handle, but he beat me to it and closed the door hard caging me with his arms, his body and that impossibly hard cock of his pressed against me.
"Do you really want me to leave Alyssa?" he whispered huskily in my ear.
I nodded, not trusting myself to speak.
"I missed you," he said gently, his lips brushing over my cheek.
"Is that why you didn't call me?" I whispered back, my eyes closed so that I couldn't see his eyes.
"I was scared to call you."
"What? Why?"
"Because I care what you think about me, and I have never cared what anyone thought about me before."
"You mean what other women thought about you?"
He sighed. "Ok, I have never cared what any other woman thought of me. You know too much Alyssa. I have never revealed that much of myself to anyone."
I turned around to face him and that was my downfall. His eyes stared into mine and I was lost.
"All that you have revealed I have kept to myself Xavier. I would never tell anyone. I am not perfect myself, as you know when I also revealed myself to you," I whispered my mouth so very close to his. "It's what people do when they are intimate with each other, and I don't mean having sex. We spent time together, special time but then you just immediately backed off. I felt that. I saw it your eyes. You detached yourself from me, from us, from all that had happened between us."
"I know. I'm an idiot. I hated myself but somehow, I couldn't stop it happening."
"It hurt me."

"I am sorry I hurt you, Alyssa." His eyes implored me to understand, and I did. I knew about demons and Xavier had more than most. "Let me make it up to you."

He traced a fingertip over my lips. I opened my mouth slightly and he traced the inside of my lips. God, that was so sexy and such a turn on. He pushed his thumb in my mouth gently and I sucked on it with my tongue and lips. His eyes closed and he moaned.

"Fuck, what are you trying to do to me Alyssa?" he asked and pulled me to him crushing his lips onto mine and pushing his tongue into my mouth. There was nothing soft and gentle about this kiss, it was hard and demanding and could only ever lead to one thing. He slid his hand into my pyjama bottoms and probing fingers reached between my legs. He groaned against my mouth when those same fingers found the inevitable wetness. He yanked at the waistband and pulled my bottoms down. They fell to my ankles, and I kicked them away. He pulled my pyjama top over my head and kissed my neck as soon as my flesh was available to him. His hands were caressing me, his mouth was insistent, and I could do nothing but surrender. But I needed answers first and, with all the willpower I could muster, I pushed him away with my hands on his hard chest. We stared at each other. His eyes were devouring me and our deep breathing the only sound in the room.

"Why didn't you call me when you got a copy of the interview from Harriet?"

"That I know is unforgivable. I should have. I read it and was blown away by how you portrayed me. For once I even liked myself."

"It was the truth and had nothing to do with...." I stalled. "Well with whatever is going on between us."

He smiled. "What is going on between us Alyssa?"

"You tell me."

"It's kind of hard to have this conversation when we are both standing here in our underwear."

"Don't do that Xavier. I want you to tell me what *this* is."

He raised an eyebrow and then closed his eyes and let out a deep breath. "More than just...fucking. I want us, this to be exclusive.

After Paris

I want you all to myself. I don't want Robert or anyone else near you."

I smiled at that, and he smiled back. He knew Robert obviously didn't exist.

"Are you saying you would like to have a relationship with me?" I asked tentatively.

He mulled that one over for a few seconds. "I guess I am."

"Like boyfriend and girlfriend?"

He winced a bit at that but then smiled. "Yes."

"Ok. That's acceptable."

"Acceptable?" he rolled his eyes. "Are you for real?"

I giggled and his eyes darkened with desire.

"Just one question girlfriend," he said, his eyes travelling over my body. "Where on earth did you get those knickers from? Your grandma?"

"Ha fucking ha," I replied with a reluctant grin pulling at my lips. "I was going for the comfort factor. Didn't know a sex maniac was going to come around and ravish me."

He grinned. "Remind me to take you lingerie shopping."

I looked down at my underwear. They were nude colour cotton and a tiny bit baggy, but they weren't that bad. Staring into his eyes, I hooked my thumbs into the elastic and pulled them slowly down, until they fell to my ankles, and I kicked them aside.

"Better?" I asked.

"Come here Alyssa," he said in a voice that had my insides melting.

I walked towards him slowly and he reached out and pulled me to him, his hands wrapped around both of my wrists. He pushed me against the door and with his good hand, held my wrists above my head. His mouth dropped to my neck, and he kissed me there, pushing his hard body against mine.

"You are so beautiful," he said, and his breath was hot on my skin.

"Did you really miss me?" I whispered.

"More than you will ever know," he answered, and I believed him.

I left my hands above my head as he let go of my wrists and lowered his mouth to my breasts, sucking on one whilst gently caressing the other. He stopped momentarily to pull off his boxers and then he crushed against me, and I felt the velvety hard length of his cock against my belly as he grabbed my hips and lifted me up allowing me to wrap my legs around him. The tip of his cock nudged at my opening, and I pushed my hips towards him. I wanted him inside me so much.

"Fuck," he whispered. "No condoms."

My eyes flew open. "What?"

"Seems like the sex maniac forgot the condoms…"

"I'm taking birth control," I whispered, and he raised his head to look at me. "I trust you, Xavier."

"I've never had sex without a condom…are you sure you want to?"

I nodded. "Yes." I had no hesitation whatsoever.

His eyes never left mine as he entered me with one hard push of his hips. I moaned loudly, the feel of him was beautiful. He was so big and felt so good. I wound my arms around his neck and cradled his head into my neck as he began to thrust into me over and over. He was so good…so good.

"Oh God, oh God Alyssa, you feel so fucking good," he said against my skin in between kisses. I was too in the moment to answer him, and I could feel my control beginning to go.

"Xavier," I breathed.

"I know baby, I know. Just let go…let go…" He pushed hard up inside me, and my orgasm bloomed, as I clung to Xavier's shoulders and my back arched off the door. It was deep and it was intense and all I could do was go with it as Xavier held me. My body pulsed and jerked against his as he watched me.

"So beautiful," he murmured as he began to pump into me again, softly at first knowing I was still tender, but gradually building up speed as he chased his own release. He came hard and fast, and he cried out with his head thrown back and then he was kissing me tenderly on the lips as for the first time, I felt his hot seed spurting inside me. We clung to each other, our foreheads together and once again our deep breathing was the only sound in the room.

CHAPTER SEVENTEEN

Xavier

I woke up to the delicious aroma of bacon wafting around in the air. Without opening my eyes, I tapped the place next to me and it was still warm but empty. I sat up and then immediately lay back down as the dizziness took over. My head was throbbing a bit and so was my hand. I hoped that dick head felt worse than me this morning. I sat up again and looked around for my boxers. They were on the floor and as I bent down to pick them up, I groaned. And this is the reason I do not get drunk anymore. I pulled my boxers on and stood up. OK, standing is better and so I made my way down the stairs following smell of the bacon.

Alyssa was standing at the hob in her kitchen, her back to me. She had a short, silky pink robe on and looked lovely. I leant against the door jamb and watched her for a while. The faint recollection of me asking her to be my girlfriend in the early hours of this morning popped into my head and I mulled that one over for a few seconds and then decided that even in the cold light of day, I actually didn't mind that scenario.
She turned and saw me and jumped slightly but then smiled.

"Good morning!" She beamed.

I smiled despite that required way too many facial muscles and made my head spin. "Morning."

"Headache still?" she asked reaching into a cupboard and taking out a box. She filled a glass with water. "Come and sit down and take these." She popped two capsules onto the breakfast island with the water next to it.

I sat down and took the capsules, drinking them down with the water.

"How's the hand?" she asked walking around to me. She took my right hand in hers and studied it. "Does it hurt?"

"Like a bitch," I replied as I winced trying to straighten it.

"Gabe says you broke Theo's nose," she said keeping her eyes on my hand.

"If I did, he deserved it. His pretty boy face will be much more interesting now."

She sighed loudly. "Xavier I am worried. He will press charges you know. That's just how he is."

"Let him. I don't really give a shit. He's a bully and he needed that punch from me years ago. I was only too happy to oblige now."

"I get that I really do, but you are no longer schoolboys who will be put in detention for an hour after having a scrape. This is serious. The police have probably been called and quite frankly I am surprised they haven't already knocked on my door asking where you are."

"Just as long as they come after my breakfast, then that is fine with me. Have you cooked me breakfast by the way? I think I am already beginning to take you for granted, seeing as you are now my girlfriend," I wiggled my eyebrows at her.

She laughed. "I wondered if you remembered that. Yes, I have everything ready. I hope you're hungry?"

"I'm starving," I grinned, grabbing her hand just as she went to walk away and pulled her close to me. "But first a kiss?"

She leant down and kissed my lips softly, her hands on each side of my face and then she pulled back and looked straight into my eyes. "I hope Eduardo sorts his mess out. I don't think I would like to think of you in prison."

After Paris

"It won't go that far Alyssa. The bastard will probably take me to court, and I will have to pay a shed load of money to him, and you know what...it will still be worth it."
"Let's hope so. Now would you like tea or coffee?"

My mobile rang just after we have finished eating a very well-cooked tasty breakfast together. Alyssa and I both look at each other. I turned my phone over to see who it was calling.
"Eduardo," I answered. "Good morning!" I could see Alyssa looking at me with concern etched across her beautiful features.
"Do you want the good news or the bad news?" Eduardo asked cutting to the chase.
I raised an eyebrow. "Give me the bad."
"He's going for assault and battery. He wants to see you in court Xavier. You broke his nose, and he is so angry he is willing to let the world know he was knocked out by you to get his own back."
I sighed. "Ok. That's fine. What's the good news?"
"The cute little waitress is willing to stand up and say that he came over and began the fight with us. She is at university and let's just say her observations have been rewarded. If I can swing that then it will be self-defence, although that will be hard to prove seeing as you were the only one to throw a punch. They are bound to get the CCTV footage of the incident and although he was aggressive, it was only verbally."
"What are we looking at here?" I asked sitting back in my chair and trying to avoid Alyssa's eyes.
"Worst case scenario?"
I nodded. "Yes."
"You get a massive fine in court and have all the hoo-hah that goes with it. Our defence will be that you were provoked and threw the punch in self-defence. To be honest it all depends how it goes on the day. I will prepare as much as I can. Hopefully it won't go that far, and we can settle out of court. He is hurting, not only his face but his pride. He is not going away easily."
"What else can we do? Just do your best Eduardo and then I will take whatever I have to." My tone is one of resignation. I punched him and he deserved it but no law in the land is going to give me that.

"It will be fine. I have a few ideas up my sleeve. Where are you anyway? Gabe said that the cab didn't take you home last night."

"With Alyssa," I said raising my eyes to hers for the first time since getting on the phone. Her eyes are all wide and filled with worry.

"Thank fuck for that," Eduardo laughed. "Now we don't have to put up with your drinking anymore."

I rolled my eyes. "Yes ok. Thanks for that. See you later bud."

I switched off my phone and put it on the table.

"Tell me," She said softly.

I shook my head. "Its fine. Eduardo has it all under control."

"Xavier, you need to start opening up to me. We are now a couple are we not? I want to know what is going on."

I looked at her and saw her eyes blazing. She's right of course. Our 'relationship' should incur some sort of trust and understanding, and I am going to have to start to share things with her, things I have for years just solved or sorted out on my own.

"There's good and bad," I started off and her eyes are glued on my face. "He is pressing charges against me for assault and battery. Eduardo says Constantine just wants his day in court to take out his revenge out on me in some way. He has always hated me and now he hates me even more."

"It's all my fault," she said staring down at her tea.

I shook my head again. "Alyssa. It's not your fault, ok? He had it coming anyway." I got up and noted that at least my head had stopped spinning even if my hand was still sore. I took her hands in mine and pulled her out of her chair and into my arms.

"I want us to forget all about that idiot and have a nice day together, ok?"

She sighed. "I can't Xavier. I must work today. My book is almost finished, and I need to edit it and get it sent off to the publishers."

I understood her work ethic and bit back my disappointment that she couldn't spend the day with me. "You're right. I have some work I need to catch up on too. Dinner with me tonight?"

She smiled and nodded. "I would love that."

"I may even cook for you…"

"What?" she laughed. "Don't tell me you cook as well? I have

After Paris

totally lucked out with my new boyfriend."

"I am half French you know and what do the French love almost as much as sex? The answer is food."

"Hmmm, sex and food. What more could a girl want?" She reached up and kissed my neck.

"I don't have to start work just yet…" She kissed me again and I felt the stirring of arousal, which went right from my lips down to my toes. Her hand reached down and stroked me through the material of my boxers, and I was full on hard in two seconds flat.

"Think I have unfinished business to attend to," she whispered huskily and went down on her knees taking my boxers with her. My cock sprang free, and she looked up at my face with heavily lidded eyes and licked her lips. I moaned and she hadn't even put those lips anywhere near me yet.

She took the base in her hand and then licked the head of my engorged member. I resisted the urge to hold her head and push myself into that hot, soft mouth of hers. I closed my eyes so that I didn't have that visual of her with my cock in her mouth, because that would seriously push me over all my limits. I felt her tongue tracing along the whole length of me and then she took the tip in her mouth and her mouth was so soft and wet it took all my willpower not to thrust my hips. She worked the base with her hand and slowly licked and sucked me with her mouth and I was in complete heaven.

Holy shit. I looked down at her and her eyes were closed as she worked her magic on me. Her rhythm was perfect, and it felt so good. Her lips sucked up and down as her head moved and I couldn't help but pump into her mouth just a bit and she opened her eyes and looked up at me.

"Alyssa…." I hissed as she upped the rhythm of her hand and mouth, and I could feel myself losing control. "If you keep doing that, I won't be able to control myself…I can't hold on."

She took her mouth from me and met my eyes full on. "I don't want you to hold on."

Her mouth went back around me, and I pushed forward. I knew I was big and that it was hard for a woman to take me fully but she seemed to accept whatever I was doing and so I pumped a little more. The sucking got stronger, the lips got softer and her hand on its own could have made me come, but all three together just about blew my mind and I came hard in her mouth. My hips jerked as for the second time in a few hours I came inside of her.

Sitting at my desk a few hours later and I still had that image in my mind. I was supposed to be looking at latest portfolios and just couldn't seem to concentrate. I had also received a call from the police asking me about the night before and telling me I had to present myself to my local station with my lawyer within the next few days. I rang Eduardo and he didn't seem concerned, just said it was standard procedure and of course he would accompany me.

I also had to attend the photo shoot for the interview. It was set up for tomorrow. I decided to read the interview again and found my email with the story attached. She really was a good writer. She had not veered away from the fact I was considered a playboy but had shown my other accomplishments alongside it, she had written about my parents without focusing on them or my relationship with them, or lack of relationship in the case of my father. She had made the endless question and answer sessions seem like interesting conversations and had filled in between the lines with her own opinions and little anecdotes on my character and lifestyle. It was good. She was good and she was also by far the hottest woman I had ever met. Our relationship had taken a step forward and I was happy it had, happy that she was now my girlfriend. Still had to tell Eduardo and Gabe but also needed to get comfortable with it myself, live with it for a while. But for the first time in a long time, I felt content. My phone pinged and I reached out to look at the screen. It was from Alyssa.

Sitting here thinking I may have made a mistake….

I grinned and tapped my reply.

Oh? What mistake would that be?
The three dots appeared immediately.

After Paris

I should have taken you up on your offer to spend the day with you x.

I typed my reply.

We have this evening. I can't wait to see you. xoxo.

The minute I pressed send I cringed inwardly. Shit, I am turning into a lovesick teenager. I even put kisses and hugs on the end of it. My phone pings back straight away and I look at the message.

Hugs and kisses? I am grinning like a Cheshire cat. Who are you and what have you done with Xavier Montgomery? xoxo

I laughed out loud at that. She is taking the piss out of me, but I like it. I like to think I am man enough to laugh at myself now and then. It pings again.

I like it. (p.s. still grinning) xoxo

I shook my head, a stupid grin on my own face too and typed my reply.

See you later Miss James....no hugs and kisses this time.... will deliver in person...

There was a knock on my door and Estelle put her head around.
"Hey Mr. Montgomery, you asked me to tell you when Tim is back in his office. His PA just called to let me know that he is back from his meeting now."
"Thanks Estelle. I'll pop and see him. You remember I won't be in tomorrow; I have that photo shoot at *Aristocrat* Magazine."
"I have it in my diary," she smiled and turned to leave.
"Estelle, I think after I have seen Tim I am taking the rest of the day off. I have some errands I need to run. Please leave early too if you have finished all your work."
"Thank you, Mr. Montgomery, and I hope you have a good

evening." She closed the door behind her.

I looked at my watch. I would nip and see Tim quickly and then go and do some shopping for tonight. I could safely say that I had never cooked a meal for a woman before. This was a first. I had cooked a lot with my mother when I was growing up as she loved to cook. Our kitchen in her villa in Monaco was always a hive of activity and sometimes we even ventured out to the local markets to get fresh produce, my mother was always heavily disguised to stop people recognising her which used to make me laugh. Once she had dressed as a gipsy woman, and had even got into character, which was hilarious. Tonight, I was going to try and recreate some of my mother's recipes for Alyssa and looking forward to it too.

After Paris

CHAPTER EIGHTEEN

Xavier

I opened the door to Alyssa at 7.30pm and immediately pulled her into my arms. She smelt so sweet and tasted even sweeter as I kissed her softly. I aimed to save all the passion for later.
"Mmmh, something smells good," she said smiling up at me as I slipped her coat from her shoulders. Underneath she had on a soft woollen dress in a nude kind of colour and caramel suede knee high boots. She looked beautiful. From behind her back, she pulled out a bottle of red wine. It was French and one of my favourites too.
"I didn't know what we were having to eat but I knew you liked this wine. I had to search for it. I found it in a small wine merchant near to where I live. The owner said I had very good taste" she smiled and held it out to me.
"I love this wine and it will go very well with what we are having for dinner," I took hold of her hand and led her through the lounge and into the kitchen. "You look beautiful by the way, and I apologise for my attire, but I get so hot when I am cooking."
"It smells divine. I can't believe you cooked it all yourself. Tell me the truth…did you have a chef come in and cook for you?"
I gave her my best affronted look and held my hand over my heart. "That is just hurtful."
She smiled and shook her head. "Ok. I believe you. I admit I am impressed."
"I give her private jets and five-star hotels rooms, and she is

impressed by homemade Boeuf Bourguignon. If only I had known...." I rolled my eyes as she laughed. I pulled out a bar stool for her to sit and then went to the fridge. "What would you like to drink?"

"Just something light and fruity," she replied as she sat crossing her legs.

"Pouilly Fumé?" I asked bringing a bottle of said wine out of the fridge.

"Sounds amazing," she breathed.

I smiled to myself as I poured her a glass. I have a feeling I could say anything in French and Alyssa would just swoon, and I know she is not the swoony type.

"So have you told anyone about us yet?" she asked as we clinked glasses.

I shook my head. "Not yet. This is a big deal for me you know. I've never had a girlfriend before."

Amusement glittered in her eyes. "Are you embarrassed to tell your friends?"

I took a big gulp of wine "I am going to get it in the neck from those two believe me but only because I think they both had money on me holding out the longest."

"Are you regretting it already?"

"No," the word is out of my mouth with no hesitation whatsoever. I shook my head to reaffirm it. "I am glad I found you again, both of you."

She sipped her wine and watched me carefully over the rim of her glass. "Do you regret that night in Masquerade?"

"What? No. I just regret that I didn't know it was you."

"Me too. I was so close to revealing myself to you," she looked me in the eye. "But it was so hot and sexy, wasn't it? The mask thing...and not knowing."

I don't know why but even talking about the night in Masquerade is turning me on big time and I feel the stirring of desire in the pit of my stomach.

"It was very hot. I admit I was totally out of my comfort zone, until I saw you and then it all seemed to make sense," I reached out and took her glass from her fingertips and placed it on the countertop. "I didn't even know it was you and yet I felt the pull

After Paris

towards you almost immediately."
"Like now?" she breathed.
I pulled her towards me still on her bar stool and ran my hands up her thighs under the soft material of her dress. I heard her small intake of breath, saw her eyes flutter, and her lips part. I can't seem to control myself at all when she is near me.
"Like now and like always when I see you," I whispered against the soft skin of her neck. "But I have slaved over a hot oven all afternoon making you dinner and so I am going to reluctantly refrain from taking this further...for now."
"I admire your willpower," she replied running her hand through my hair at the nape of my neck. I loved it when she did that, it made me feel like she was staking her claim on me.
"Where you're concerned my willpower only lasts so long and so I suggest we eat," I planted a quick kiss on her lips and pulled away. I helped her down and led her to the dining room. I had set the table for two and had even bought candles which I lit now. I held a chair for her to sit down.
"*Mademoiselle?*"
She grinned at me as she took her seat. "I can't believe that you have done all of this for me."
"Well, just to let you into a little secret, you are the first woman I have ever cooked for, apart from my mother."
"Have any of your women ever been here to your house?"
"They are not my women," I grinned. "And no for your information. I have never invited any women here before."
"Wow! I'm starting to feel special here Mr. Montgomery," She smiled at me sexily over the rim of her wine glass and I watched intently as her luscious lips took a sip. "First girlfriend, first woman you have cooked for, the first invited into your bachelor pad."
"A day of firsts..." I let my words trail as I poured some more wine for her. "And now I must leave and go back to the kitchen. The soup should be just about ready."
"Soup as well?" Holy shit. I am truly being spoilt."
"Sit back and relax *Mademoiselle*. I am here to serve."

Alyssa

I sat back and relaxed and sipped my wine. My heart was beating fast in my chest and my stomach was doing somersaults. When Xavier admitted that I was the first woman he had cooked for and invited to his house, I cannot deny that I felt thrilled and a tiny bit nervous. I had played it cool, but inside I was a mess. What the hell was going on here? Could it be that he was beginning to feel the same about me as I did about him? He was being the perfect boyfriend and, yes, saying that he was my boyfriend gave me goose bumps all over. Seeing him this evening had made my heart flip as he was dressed casually in tight faded jeans and a white t shirt. It was a simple outfit but on him it was so hot. The jeans were tight and showed off his long legs and the t-shirt clung to all the parts of his torso that it should cling to without being obvious, showcasing his muscly arms to perfection. I can't believe he apologised for how he was dressed, for me he looked so sexy it was sending my hormones into overdrive.

He came back into the dining room with two small round white bowls. He placed one before me and put one at his own place setting. It smelt so good and looked wonderful.

"Voila!" he said standing back proudly "French Onion soup with grilled brioche and gruyere cheese."

"This looks amazing," I said picking up my spoon eager to start.

"It's my mother's recipe. In fact, everything tonight is from the days when I was growing up in France and the happy times spent in my mother's kitchen cooking with her."

"Your mother was a good cook? I thought all glamourous movie stars would be.... well too glamourous to cook."

"My mother loved to cook. I think she truly found her real self when she stood in her kitchen with bare feet and an apron on cooking her recipes. I loved it when we cooked together," He sat opposite me and poured me and himself some more wine.

"Well, I think that is a lovely thing to do. And it looks like your mother has taught you well. You are a man of hidden talents. I wish I had known this before I wrote the article."

After Paris

"There are some things that are best kept secret don't you think?" he smiled across the table at me. "But you have somehow managed to find more out about me than most. I somehow seem to just tell you things...things even my best friends don't know about me."
I smiled. "That is because I am such a good listener...I tend to let people just talk and don't ask too many questions."
We looked at each other for a long moment before I looked down at my bowl. "I am going to eat now as I can't wait another moment."
The food was delicious. After the soup Xavier had made us Boeuf Bourguignon served with delicious, crushed potatoes and fresh vegetables. The dessert was crème brûlée and then he brought out fresh coffee to finish.
I sat back and sipped my coffee and marvelled once again that he had cooked all of this himself. I had meant what I said earlier that he was man of hidden talents but also some very obvious ones too, like how he was looking at me now. Like he hadn't just eaten a three-course meal and he could devour me.
"Thank you," I said as I tried to ignore his eyes full of longing. "The meal was superb."
"If I were you, I would stop talking about food and get yourself over here right now," he said in a really, really deep and sexy voice. "The chef would like you to show him some appreciation."
How could a girl resist a man who says something like that? Well, I couldn't and stood up and walked around to him very slowly. He looked up at me with those beautiful eyes of his and added in a soft voice. "Take the dress off."
"I thought you liked this dress."
"I do. But I would like to see you without it."
My dress was a soft cashmere knit and so I reached down to the hem and pulled it up over my head in one smooth movement. My underwear was caramel lace. I saw his eyes ignite with passion as they trailed over my body. I should be used to him by now, used to the way he looks at me, used to the way he consumes me with his hot steamy stare. But I find I am not, and it still sends shivers all the way through my body.
"Turn around Miss James," he said in his husky whisper. "I want

to see all of you."

Oh. My. God. This man. The things his voice and his eyes do to me. He hasn't even touched me, and I know I am wet.... embarrassingly so. I turned around slowly. I heard a soft moan emanate from him and when I turned back and looked into his eyes the calm blue sea had become a storm.

He reached out and pulled me to him, his hands on my hips. His lips kissed my belly and my breath caught in my throat. They trailed across my skin and where they touched, they burnt. His hand cupped between my legs, and he stroked me through the scrap of lace that was so flimsy that it may as well not be there. I writhed against his hand as he groaned out loud.

"Your panties are soaked," he said looking up at me.

"You know why," I whispered back.

"Take them off."

I laughed, nervous and yet excited at the same time and hooked two fingers each side of the lace and shimmied them over my hips and down my thighs and finally over my boots. I dangle them from my finger and let them drop to the floor not once taking my eyes from his.

He raised his eyebrows, and my fingers go directly to the fastening of my bra and in two seconds that is also in my fingertips. I dropped that to the floor too. Xavier's eyes leave mine only to roam over my now very naked body and he obviously likes what he sees as his eyes have gone that stormy sea colour again. He gently traced the tattoo on my shoulder with his fingertips.

"I totally get the butterfly story now," he said his eyes coming back to mine. "You were freed from that claustrophobic relationship with the dick head."

I nodded. "Had it done in Paris."

"It's all making sense," He stood up and pulled his t-shirt over his head. God, I would never get tired of looking at that body. He popped the button on his jeans and pulled them down his long legs and flung them on the floor. With the heat pooling in my stomach, I watched as he lowered his boxers and that magnificent cock of his sprung free.

Then he walked towards me and picked me up like I weighed

nothing and sat me on the dining table, pushing all the remnants of our meal out of the way.
"My boots..." I muttered.
"Leave them on," His voice was deep and commanding.
He pushed me back and when my bare skin touched on the cool wood my back arched. He pulled me towards him so that my backside was near the edge of the table.
"I need to fuck you Alyssa," He looked at me with hooded lust filled eyes. "And it's going to be hard and fast..."
I nodded not even trusting myself to speak.
Staring into my eyes he thrust his hips forward and entered me hard. I cried out, throwing back my head as he began to move inside me. For a moment my mind took in the scene, me naked on the dining table, my legs spread wide as a naked beautiful specimen of a man pummelled into me like there was no tomorrow. His eyes were closed as he thrust his slim hips hard into the very core of me. This was crazy, wild, and so hot and sexy and just what we both needed. There had been no need for any foreplay because the whole run up to this moment had been the foreplay. This was pure unadulterated sex at its finest. I looked up into his eyes and they were intense like he was looking into my soul. He reached out and cupped the back of my neck in his hand and pulled my mouth up to meet his, his lips crushing on mine in a kiss that was as demanding and forceful as the movement of his body on my body.
"Oh God, Xavier," I murmured as he tore his lips from mine for a moment.
"I know babe," he whispered back huskily. "I love being inside you...you feel so good Alyssa."
Xavier took me way beyond any boundaries that I had ever been sexually, and it just felt natural with him. Perhaps it was because I was in love with him and that I trusted him and so was relaxed with him. I just knew that I had never felt this with anyone else ever.
I leant back onto the table and Xavier's hands moved to my breasts, and he cupped them in his hands, caressing them and running his palms over the nipples which made me writhe in pleasure. Then his hands moved down to my hips which he

gripped onto as he thrust inside me. I lay back and met each one of his thrusts with one of my own and couldn't help the moans that escaped from my lips.

"Tell me you are near Alyssa; I can't hold back any longer…" his voice was deep and husky with desire "I want to come inside you…"

His words went straight to that place between my legs, and I felt myself begin to lose any sort of control that I thought I had and, gripping on to the side of the table with both hands, I let go as my orgasm washed over me like a tidal wave.

"Xavier…." I moaned.

"Oh God, Alyssa…" his back arched, and he threw back his head and he cried out as he came deep inside me.

He fell on top of me, his breathing as deep and laboured as my own as held me close, his head resting on my chest.

My hands went to his hair, and I gently ran my fingers through the silky strands as we lay there for a few moments catching our breath and just being in the aftermath of some really intensive sex.

He kissed my stomach and I smiled. I felt so close to him in that moment.

"Are you ok?" he asked raising his eyes to mine.

I nodded smiling down at him.

"I want you to stay the night," he said his eyes still holding mine. Then he smiled "And before you say anything, yes you are the first woman I have ever asked to stay and to be in my bed."

"A lot of firsts today," I grinned as he kissed his way slowly up to my lips and planted a soft kiss upon them.

"Don't get too damned sure of yourself Miss James," he grinned back and leaned down to kiss me again.

CHAPTER NINETEEN

Xavier

Eduardo met me at the police station the next morning. The police had to charge me with assault and told me that the court would be sending me papers of when to attend and how things were going forward. Eduardo looked over everything and agreed that all was in order and very much what was expected. Then we went for brunch.

"So," Eduardo said after we had ordered. "How are things going with Alyssa?"

My mind went back to this morning and the feeling of waking up next to Alyssa, her warm soft body curled around mine, another first for me…. waking up with a woman in my bed. I recalled her sleepy smile when I kissed her awake and then, as if we had not had enough of each other during the night, the steamy, intense sex session that followed, our bodies automatically knowing what the other wanted that sated both of our needs. Then we had showered together, soaping each other and it was only the impending meeting I had with Eduardo that stopped me taking her again. Alyssa James was getting under my skin in a way that no other woman had.

I grinned at him. "It's going well."

Eduardo grinned and leant back in his chair. "So, is she 'The One'?"

"Well, she's the only one I have asked to be my girlfriend…"

"Fuck me!" Eduardo laughed just as the waitress returned with our drinks. He looked up at her sheepishly knowing she had just heard that "Sorry."

The waitress smiled flirtatiously, and Eduardo smiled back but waited until she had placed our coffees in front of us and left before he carried on.

"Are you dating?"

"We're not fifteen for crying out loud. We are seeing each other on an exclusive basis. Put it this way if anyone asked if she was my girlfriend I would say yes."

"Holy shit! I never thought I would see the day."

"She stayed at my place last night. I dropped her home this morning."

"What? You had a woman in your sacred bachelor pad?" He sat back and stared at me grinning. "Now I know she is special."

I took a sip of my coffee. "I must admit that I have no idea where this is going, because as you know I don't do relationships, but I like her in my life. I like knowing she is there. Oh shit! Listen to me. Do I sound like a pussy?"

Eduardo grinned again. "Sounds like you are smitten my man."

"Fuck, I think I am."

"How the mighty have fallen."

I shrugged. "If it can happen to me, it can happen you too my friend."

Eduardo laughed. "No chance. I am having way too much of a good time but if you want my thoughts on this, I think Alyssa is a beautiful, intelligent woman, although what she sees in you, I don't really understand."

"Yeah, fuck off," I laughed.

"And in a way you have me to thank for being Cupid."

"How are you working that one out?"

"If I hadn't persuaded you to go that club...."

"I met her before the club. Remember? At the café?"

"Yes, but the night in the club only reaffirmed your attraction and connection."

I snort a laugh. "Not entirely your handy work but ok, I give you that. Perhaps that should be your name at the club. Cupid."

He laughed with me. "That actually suits me."

"Do you still go to the club?"

After Paris

"Xavier...you know I can't talk about that."
"All those fucking rules and regulations.... plus, that night was kinky. Not comfortable watching other people having sex I must admit. If I hadn't have met Alyssa, I probably would have left early."
Eduardo raised an eyebrow. "Yes, ok vanilla with sprinkles man. There are one hundred and one other flavours to try you know."
I laughed. "You forgot the chocolate sauce."
"Whatever floats your boat mate, I am just glad you have found a good woman to ground you a bit."
I sipped my coffee and smiled. Yes, Alyssa grounded me and for the first time in a long time I felt that contentment had crept into my life. She almost filled all the voids...almost.
"Yes, well after this I am off to a photo shoot for Alyssa's article."
Eduardo shook his head. "Such a hard life. Still, I suppose someone must do it!"

The photo shoot went well. The photographer was a woman, Jenni Brooks and she was easy on the eyes dressed in a black leather mini skirt and knee-high boots. We chatted a bit at first whilst her assistants got the outfits ready, and I could tell she was flirting with me. She was cute but she wasn't Alyssa.
"So, Xavier what's your status at the moment?" she asked as she snapped happily away.
"Status?" I asked frowning slightly.
"Yes, as in significant other? Is there someone?"
"Yes," I replied with no hesitation whatsoever. "I have a girlfriend."
She raised both eyebrows as she studied me over the top of her camera. "Oh?"
I smiled. "You're surprised?"
"I am a bit I must admit. I heard you were a bit of a playboy, not into relationships."
"My past life."
"But once a playboy....?" She let her words trail away and held my eyes for a long moment, the invitation there if I wanted it. I was an old hand at this. I knew when a woman was interested,

and Jenni definitely was. The thing was, I wasn't.
I shook my head. "Afraid to disappoint but my old life is well and truly history. I have a girlfriend and she is someone that I would like to hold on to for the foreseeable future."
RSVP - Sorry not interested.
The light dimmed in Jenni's eyes, but she forced a smile anyway. "Lucky girl."
"I am the lucky one believe me."
Jenni smiled and then snapped her eyes away from me and called to one of the assistants. "Next outfit please."

Later that night as Alyssa and I lay in each other's arms, both sated and sleepy after I had worshipped her body twice in succession, that sense of contentment returned and curled around me just like her soft, warm limbs.
"How did the photo shoot go today?" Alyssa asked.
I shrugged. "Ok. I guess. The photographer was happy."
"Which photographer did they use?"
"Jenni Brooks," I felt her tense beside me.
"Did you find her attractive?"
I rolled my lips, holding back a smile. "I didn't notice really. She had a mini skirt on and boots."
Alyssa leant upon her elbow and scowled down at me. "So, you noticed what she was wearing?"
"Well, it would have been a bit hard not to."
"Admit you found her attractive."
I shrugged again. "She was ok. Not really my type to be honest. Bit too in your face."
She pulled away from me. "Did she flirt with you?"
"Would you be jealous if I said she did a bit? She asked me if I had a girlfriend."
"And?"
I grinned. "I said that I did have a girlfriend and she is the really jealous type and so she needed to back off."
"I can't believe her! How is that being professional? Oh my God!"
I laughed and pulled her into my arms again. "Alyssa calm down. I told her I had a girlfriend and that I was happy with said

girlfriend. I also told Eduardo by the way."
I felt her relax slightly, mollified by my words and she wound her arms back around me too.
"You told Eduardo about us?" she said softly as she nuzzled her lips against my neck.
"Mm-hmm," I murmured.
"Was he happy for you?"
"Yeah, after he took the piss out of me for a while. He says I have found the woman to ground me."
"Xavier, I never want to change you. I like you just the way you are."
"I know but I was living a lie. I was starting to get bored with my way of life. It had all become a bit superficial. Partying and the never-ending round of...." I was about to say women but somehow that didn't seem appropriate and respectful towards this gorgeous woman in my arms.
I felt her mouth curve into a smile against the skin on my neck.
"Women?" she filled in.
I sighed. "Yeah. Women," I paused hating that I was bringing up my wayward past. "Sorry Alyssa..."
She leant up on her elbow again and placed a fingertip to my lips. "It's ok. I know what your life was like before you met me. I don't want you to feel like you need to hide stuff."
I frowned. "Yes, but I don't want to rub your nose in it either. Those women meant nothing to me. Some of them were decent women to be honest that didn't need to be treated like I treated them. I am not proud of how I behaved. I spent most of my twenties being wild and reckless. I was angry and hurt for most of my teenage years and that just kind of carried on into my twenties. I needed to let go of that man."
"And do you think you have let that version of you go?"
"Almost...."
"But not quite?" She leant her chin on my chest and looked up at me wriggling her eyebrows. "I hope you don't mean the conveyer belt of women?"
"Oh, good God, no. That part has taken a back seat. No, I guess I was still talking about the hurt and angry side."
"Courtesy of your father no doubt?"

I nodded but remained silent. The one fly in the ointment was the estrangement between my father and me. As a child I blamed myself for what happened to Guillaume. As a grown man I had knew that it had been an accident, a terrible traumatic accident. What I couldn't understand was how my father, a grown man, had blamed me, a child. It had taken me years of internal conflict to arrive at this conclusion but deep down I think I had always known and that hurt. It hurt that he had pushed me away and it hurt that he had blamed me for an accident. Over the years I had played that day over and over in my head and I knew that I had swam faster than ever that day to get to him and delved under the murky water three or four times before I found him. That day had been traumatic for me too and I had lost my little brother that I loved more than life itself. I would never fully come to terms with what happened that day but maybe it was time to stop thinking that I was the failure.

"Maybe you should finally go and meet him?" Alyssa suggested tentatively. "Talk to him …"

I shook my head vehemently. "No way. He knows where I am. He has always known where I am."

"But…"

"No!" I cut her off before she could say anymore. Her deep dark eyes stared at me.

"Ok. Sorry." She said in a quiet voice, and I immediately hated myself for allowing my father to inadvertently cause the first bit of tension between myself and Alyssa.

I pulled her up to me so that we were face to face. "Alyssa. No, I am sorry. I shouldn't take my shit out on you."

"That's ok and that's what being in a relationship is all about. I am here for you and all your shit too."

I felt a smile tugging at the corners of my lips. "All of my shit?" She grinned. "Well, yes of course. That's what all good girlfriends do."

I couldn't help but let out a small laugh and then I pulled her towards me and kissed her lips softly.

"Glad I got myself a good girlfriend then."

She kissed me long and soft, and I could feel the beginnings of the inevitable stirring in my groin area. She drew back and looked

After Paris

at me in that way that made the stirring become so much more. "Sometimes I can be bad too," she said seductively. "Really bad." "Is that so?" I whispered against her lips. "Come here and show me just how bad you can be."

Alyssa

So, Xavier and I were really in a relationship. I sat at my desk staring into space and dreaming of him. Like a lovesick schoolgirl. He made me smile just thinking about him. I wasn't surprised that Jenni Brooks hit on him, but that didn't stop my annoyance. I had seen the photos this morning, sent courtesy of Harriet, and he looked so absolutely beautiful in them that Jenni bloody Brooks had almost redeemed herself...almost. I still wanted to make it abundantly clear to her that he was mine.

Last night I had those three little words hanging on to the end of my tongue so many times and yet...and yet I could not bring myself to say them out loud. Although the barriers were breaking down, I didn't think Xavier was ready to jump from serial womanising playboy straight to loved-up boyfriend. I hated the fact that I couldn't just tell him how I was feeling but I knew he wasn't ready. The sex...well the sex was out of this world. I don't think I ever thought sex could be like that in real life...only on the pages of romance novels... but with Xavier it was like he was every romantic hero ever written rolled into one.

I had never told a man that I loved them before. My boyfriends before Theo were always on a very casual basis and then Theo...I had never loved Theo. He had me mesmerised at the beginning and I was, I suppose, overwhelmed by his infatuation with me. It was only afterwards I realised that his incessant need to know where I was all the time, was in fact down to his own deep-rooted insecurities and his very nasty jealous streak. Now, out of his claustrophobic hold, I could see it for exactly what it was, controlling and bullying behaviour. His family, although not as bad as him, were similar. Rich and privileged, they were all used to getting what they wanted and because he wanted me, they wanted me. My life in those few months while they planned our wedding was hell on earth. Lying to my parents and to Naomi was awful, even though Naomi finally caught on when I had to tell her that someone else was designing my wedding dress. She had never fully taken to Theo and had finally convinced me, during a very rare night out without him that I needed to get out of that relationship. I hadn't needed much convincing at that point I must admit. I think Naomi needs to meet Xavier. He needs to meet some of my friends too. I reached for my mobile and tap out a message.

Hi!! It's me. I was thinking of going for a drink with my friend Naomi tonight. Would you, Eduardo and Gabe like to join us? X.

I then texted Naomi to let her know and her text came back with a smiley face and a thumbs up.

My phone pinged. It was from Xavier.

Hi! I know it's you! I think that would be a great idea. I know Eduardo and Gabe will be up for it. Where would you like to meet? X.

I smiled and tapped my reply.

How about the Nickel Bar at The Ned? 7pm X.

His response came back immediately.

Great. See you there. 7pm. Look forward to it. You ok today? X.

I beamed. He was asking how I was and that made me feel all warm and fuzzy inside.

A bit sore after last night…. but so totally worth it. (Wink emoji)

After Paris

The three dots appeared as he was typing his response. I waited with a stupid grin on my face.

Would you like me to rub some cream on that for you Miss James? X.

I giggled but I was turned on at the same time and squirmed a bit in my chair. God, this was a whole new side to Xavier, and I loved it.

Yes please…am I the only one to be getting turned on by this conversation? X.

His reply pinged back.

No…. I now have to go into a very important meeting with a very distinct bulge in my trousers…X.

I laughed out loud at that.

See you later…and good luck with that meeting. Xx.

With a smile on my face, I went back to work.

CHAPTER TWENTY

Alyssa

Naomi and I arrived early at The Nickel Bar. It was 6.30pm but I needed to see her first before the guys arrived. She looked stunning in one of her own creations, a jade green fitted dress with a low v neck which showed just the right amount of cleavage without being too showy. Her caramel hued hair was in soft waves down her back, and I could see some of the men keep looking over at her as we talked at the bar. I had decided to dress in a bright red trouser suit. The trousers were tight and straight, the jacket fitted. I couldn't quite get away with wearing nothing underneath like that model in Paris, but instead had teamed it up with a white lacy camisole. My accessories were black high pumps and a black shiny bag. My hair had been washed and styled and fell in a dark shiny curtain around my shoulders.
"So," Naomi said leaning towards me. "Tell me again about Xavier's friends."
I took a sip of my mojito through the shiny red straw. "You remember Eduardo is a lawyer and Gabe is an architect. They are both so handsome and really nice too. Eduardo has that Spanish thing going on almost as dark as Xavier but not quite and Gabe has that dark blonde hair and amazing green eyes. I have never seen three such handsome men, they really are quite breath taking."

After Paris

"Oh my God, I'm quite nervous," Naomi admitted taking a sip of her own cocktail. "Tell me about you and Xavier to take my mind off it."

"Well...we are exclusive."

"What? When did this happen?"

"It's all very new. He is so amazing Naomi. I can't even begin to tell you how he makes me feel and even now just talking about him and saying his name makes me feel like some giddy schoolgirl."

She looked at me for a very long moment and then said, "How long have you been in love with him?"

I let out a laugh but could feel my skin burning and no doubt I was turning as red as my suit. Shit! She could always read me so well. Was it really that obvious? I met her eyes.

"Since Paris.... outside the café...." I said quietly.

She let out a huge sigh. "Well hallelujah, finally she admits what was so obvious."

I frowned. "Please don't tell me that I'm that obvious. Do you think that Xavier knows? I don't want to bombard him with the L word just yet."

She shook her head. "It was only obvious to me. He probably hasn't got a clue. But you shouldn't hold back on your feelings Alyssa. When you are ready to tell him, you should and if he is not ready then that is his problem."

I nodded. "I know Naomi, but he is complicated..."

"We're all complicated in our own way Alyssa. You need to tell him." She looked over my shoulder and clutched my arm. "Oh my God. I think they have arrived. Holy shit, you were so right."

I turned and saw Xavier heading towards us with Eduardo and Gabe not far behind him. They were all dressed in their work suits still and looked like three catwalk models for one of those Italian designers. Women from all sides were looking at them as they made their way through the crowd and that warm fuzzy feeling burst inside me again. Xavier reached us first and pulled me to him like he hadn't seen me for ten years and kissed me gently on the lips.

"Hi," he said when he pulled back, looking straight into my eyes.

"Hi," I said softly, and I knew I was blushing but there was nothing I could do about it.

He put his arm around my waist and smiled at Naomi "And you must be Naomi, Hi. Xavier Montgomery." He shook Naomi's hand whilst she stood a bit speechless for a moment. This was first. Naomi was never speechless.

"Hi," she smiled. "Lovely to meet you."

Gabe and Eduardo stepped forward and both kissed me on the cheek in greeting. Introductions were made with Naomi, and I watched in quiet amusement as both Gabe and Eduardo checked her out, whilst both pretending not to.

"Let's get some drinks in," Xavier said. "Usual for you guys and looks like cocktails for the ladies."

Xavier and I held back as we watched Gabe and Eduardo chatting animatedly with Naomi. She threw back her head and laughed at something one of them had said and I smiled.

"Which one do you think she'll go for?" Xavier asked.

"You know your friends better than me, who do you think is more interested in her?"

"Eduardo," he said with no hesitation whatsoever.

I narrowed my eyes. "Really? Because I would have said that Gabe has been chatting with her more and her attention seems to be on him so much more…"

"Which is exactly why it must be Eduardo. Both he and Naomi are trying to ignore each other which in conclusion means they are interested in each other."

I watched the scenario again and saw Eduardo pretending not to really be interested in Naomi, his eyes drifting around the bar, whilst his smile remained in place as he half listened to the conversation. Whereas all of Naomi's attention was on Gabe, until she thought Eduardo wasn't looking and then let her eyes wander to him but as soon as he looked at her, she switched her gaze back to Gabe.

"I do believe you are right Sherlock," I said laughing.

"Elementary my dear Watson," Xavier smiled back.

"Since when did you become so good at sussing out the psychology between men and women?"

He raised his eyebrows. "Please…you are talking to the master

After Paris

of psychological goings on between the sexes."

"Of course. How silly of me to forget," I rolled my eyes and Xavier grinned. "So do you think Eduardo will make a move on Naomi?"

"If Naomi is into hook ups and fun times then maybe he will. I don't think he is into looking for anything serious right now."

"Hmmh…that's not going to work then. Naomi is a relationship person. She doesn't do casual. Maybe she will be the one to sway him?"

Xavier pulled me close. "Like you and me?"

"Is that what you think happened?"

He pulled me even closer, wrapping his arms around my waist and pressing his lean body against me "Not so much swayed…more like bulldozed…."

My mouth fell open in mock surprise. "I can't believe you just said that!"

He laughed and then leant down and kissed me softly, yep right there in front of everyone.

"Guys…." Gabe called. "Get a room!"

Both Xavier and I grinned at that.

"Actually," he whispered. "That's not a bad idea. Shall I go and book us a room here for the night?"

"What? That's crazy. I haven't got anything with me."

"What do you need?"

I pondered that for a moment. "Em…toothbrush?"

"Easily sorted. Wait there I'm going to book us in."

I watched him walk away, along with most of the other women in the room. He was impulsive and a tad daring but that's what I loved about him. He took me right out of my comfort zone.

Naomi appeared by my side. "Where has Xavier gone? Don't tell me he really has gone to book a room?"

I nodded. "The man is unbelievable."

"That is so sexy," Naomi said her voice all breathy. "I am excited for you Alyssa. You know we had that conversation earlier…."

I nodded again.

"Well, I think tonight is the night. Tell him. You may be surprised to learn that he feels the same."

"You don't think that it's too early?"

"How can it be if you feel it?"
Gabe and Eduardo joined us before I had time to answer.
"He has gone to book you a room, hasn't he?" Eduardo asked with a smirk.
I shook my head in embarrassment. "I kind of think he has…"
Gabe burst out laughing and I almost died on the spot. Eduardo nudged him hard in the ribs. "You are such a Neanderthal Gabe! It's a very romantic gesture. Ignore the idiot, Alyssa. He just hates that he is not as smooth as Xavier."
"Speaking of which," Gabe grinned. "Here comes Mr. Smooth himself now."
We all turned to look at Xavier who was making his way through the crowd looking very pleased with his self. He beamed at us all.
"Have a good evening, guys, and Naomi. Please make sure Naomi gets home ok you two. Alyssa and I are leaving. Au revoir…" He reached for my hand, and I just managed to grab my bag as he pulled me towards the exit.
I waved over my shoulder and planted a kiss on Naomi's cheek as she raced after me, and I caught her eyes as she silently reaffirmed her message. Gabe and Eduardo were just grinning like two Cheshire cats.
As we waited for the lift, I could feel my cheeks burning.
"You know that they all now know we have booked a room to have sex, don't you?" I whispered.
Xavier grinned and squeezed my hand. "Alyssa…why do you care? They all have sex."
"I know, but I wouldn't necessarily want to know when and where they are having it."
He laughed and pulled me gently into the lift waiting until the doors had shut before he caged me in, both hands on the wall either side of my face. He pressed himself against me with his eyes staring straight into mine and I could feel his huge erection against my stomach.
"That," he whispered close to my ear. "Has been like that all day."
I reached down to run my finger along the length of him through his trousers. He groaned and grabbed my hand stopping me in my tracks.

After Paris

"If you touch me, I am not going to last five minutes."
His mouth crushed down on mine, and he hungrily plundered my mouth with his tongue leaving me gasping. The lift pinged and we reluctantly broke apart, both of us breathing erratically. With my hand still in his we almost ran along the long corridor until Xavier stopped outside a room and scanned the key. The door clicked open and before I knew it, we were inside, and his lips were on mine again as he shrugged himself out of his jacket letting it fall to the floor around our feet. His fingers unbuttoned my jacket, and he pushed it from my shoulders, and it joined his on the floor. He tore at his tie and shirt and within seconds he was bare chested. My hands skimmed over his hard lean chest and across his abs and once again I silently thanked someone up above for bestowing Xavier Montgomery upon me.
"Too many clothes on," he said between kisses. "I need you naked."
We watched each other as we stripped off and when we were both naked, our ravenous eyes appraised each other's bodies until we finally fell onto the bed where our lips crushed together, our fingers entwined, his skin was against my skin, his body pressing mine into the soft luxurious mattress as he kissed me until I didn't even remember my own name. When he finally entered me, I was beyond ready, my body treading that fine line between want and need and I knew Naomi was right. I had to tell him how I felt.

Xavier

I slowly opened my eyes and allowed my gaze to roam around the room. It was lovely, understated, and elegant, what you would expect really from a five-star establishment. I hadn't even noticed the room when we had arrived. The only thing important was to get naked together and have mind blowing sex. *Tick. Tick. Achieved.* I reached for Alyssa but to my surprise the space beside me was empty and cold and I sat up suddenly alarmed. There were no lights on anywhere, apart from the moonlight streaming in the window through the gap in the curtains. Where was she? I looked at the floor and saw her red trousers still by the bed and my heart resumed its normal beat. So, she hadn't left. I pushed the quilt back and padded barefoot and naked to the bathroom. The door was closed, and I knocked tentatively.

"Alyssa?" I called.

"Yes. I'm here."

"Can I come in?"

"I'm coming out now."

The door opened slowly, and she appeared, totally naked too. She smiled at me, but I had already caught her worried expression seconds before.

"What wrong?" I asked putting both my hands on her shoulders and making her look at me.

She shook her head. "Nothing…"

"Calling bullshit," I said trying for a smile, but none was forthcoming. "Ok. Tell me."

"Can we get back in bed at least?" she asked as she shivered slightly. "I feel a bit cold."

I followed her to the bed, and we got in wrapping the quilt around us. I reached to turn the bedside lamp on, but she caught my hand and shook her head.

"Don't. Don't turn the lights on."

I frowned. *What the hell was this all about?* "Alyssa? Tell me. I thought we shared things. Isn't that what you said? How this relationship malarkey goes…?"

"Is that you think? That this…" she gestured between us. "Is just malarkey?"

I ran a hand through my hair. *Where on earth was this conversation going?*

"No. of course not I was just saying it to lighten the mood…"

"I love you, Xavier."

Well, I didn't expect it to go there.

I stared at her for a long moment and then let out a breath that I wasn't aware I was holding. I ran my hand through my hair again nervously and then rubbed both hands over my face trying to gain some time to think what to say. Women had said they loved me before, usually during the throes of hot steamy sex and after a few bottles of the sparkling stuff but I had never ever taken it

seriously. I had got used to it over the years. All tipsy women said that during sex. Alyssa hadn't. She was saying it now while we were not having sex and we were certainly not tipsy, not even a bit. Were stone cold sober. I looked up the ceiling for a moment to try and gather my thoughts. Ok, she loved me that was good, wasn't it? Shit. I was just getting used to the boyfriend thing and now she loves me.... I take another deep breath and look at her. She looks beautiful with her bed hair and smudged make up and those deep dark eyes staring at me silently. Holy fuck and shit!
"You don't need to feel obliged Xavier to say it back....in fact please don't just say it back, not if you don't feel it. It is just how I feel...I had to tell you. I know that it's too much for you...its early in our relationship and fuck. I know I'm talking way too much. It's just that I've never told a man I love him before and well it's a big deal for me...I'll stop talking now," she clamped her lips closed and let out a huge sigh. In an ideal world I would now take her into my arms and hold her and tell her what she wanted to hear but shit, that is a big step and one I have never taken.
How the fuck do I respond to this without hurting her?
"Alyssa...." I breathe and I know I am stalling for time again.
She stared at me not saying a word waiting for me to speak.
"First of all, I want to say..." I began but she jumped up and looked around for her panties on the floor and pulled them on.
"What are you doing?"
"Going home."
"Alyssa it's three in the morning."
"I don't care."
I watched as she fastened her bra and slipped her white camisole over her head.
"Alyssa...you haven't even waited to hear what I have to say."
"I don't need to. I am absolutely mortified that I have even told you this. I am an idiot."
She pulled her trousers on and fastened them as she slipped on her shoes.
"Alyssa, please. I am so honoured that you love me..."
"No. No you're not. You are horrified and now think I am just like all the other women that have told you they love you and

don't even try and deny that because I know there must have been at least some women that have said that to you over the years."

I shrugged. "I don't care what other women have said. I only care what you say."

I watched her helplessly as she pushed her arms into her jacket, and she turned her eyes to mine.

"Now I am the one calling bullshit." She turned her back on me as she did up the buttons.

"Not fair Alyssa," I jumped out of bed and swung her around to face me. "Please don't go. Let's talk about this."

"There's nothing more to say Xavier. My soul is now bare to you, and I have handed you my heart on a platter. I have nowhere else to go."

She was right of course. She had laid herself bare to me. I needed to put this right.

"Alyssa, I have problems with being as honest as you with feelings. I have only ever loved three people and one of them died right in my arms. Then my mother wanted to die but my father made me want to die. Love has only ever brought me heartache and pain. I don't know how to love anyone, in fact I made myself a promise that I would never love anyone else ever again. I was thirteen when I made that promise and I know it was stupid but part of that is still with me because I never want to feel like that again."

"Are you saying that you could never love me?" she asked in a quiet husky voice.

Am I? Am I saying that I could never love a woman like Alyssa? I so could. Falling in love with Alyssa would be the easiest thing in the world. Looking at her now standing there before me, having laid herself bare, I could let myself fall head over heels and give her everything. But even as I thought it, I felt my stomach lurch with anxiety. I have never loved a woman before but according to my track record, loving someone means heartache and pain. It always means they leave you one way or another. Every meaningful love song ever written underlines the fact that love, whatever that means, leads to someone being hurt. I was a strong person in many ways, but with love I was one big

After Paris

fat ugly coward.
"I'm saying that I don't know and that is the honest answer."
"Well, that's it then," she whispered. "There really is nothing left to say."
She bent down and picked her bag up off the floor and walked towards the door. My heart was thumping hard in my chest; I had never felt like this before. For the first time ever, I had no idea what to say to make her stay and make it right again. I felt like I couldn't breathe. In my head I was running after her begging her not to leave but in the cold hard light of day, I stood there like a statue unable to move. I was completely numb.
She opened the door and then turned to look at me. "For the record, I am not sorry I told you I loved you because I do. That is not going to change. Even with all your past playboy shit I still love you. I especially love you because of the tragedy you went through but if you can't move on and sort things out Xavier, however you need to do that, you will never be able to be the man I want to love me back."
The door clicked shut behind her almost silently.
I sat down on the bed and felt my throat constrict. I was distraught. I had never cried since that day at the lake but shit if I didn't feel like I wanted to cry right now. *What the fuck?* She was right of course. I needed to sort my shit out and I needed to sort it out now before it was too late, and I lost the best thing that had happened to me for a long time. I reached down and pulled on my boxers and then got dressed almost as fast as I had undressed. I needed to go home and think. Think about what to do to get her back.

CHAPTER TWENTY-ONE

Xavier

It had been five days since I had heard from Alyssa. Her article on me had hit the newsstands and everyone had been raving about it. But somehow for me it all had fallen flat. Now every word she had written about me seemed like another tiny nail hammered into my heart. I remembered how feisty she had been at the beginning and our trip to Paris and all the other bits in between and I realised that I had made a terrible mistake and that was hard to admit even to myself. I realised that I had loved her since that day outside the café and the steamy night that had followed just confirmed everything.

I missed her.

In the cold hard light of day, I knew that I had been a complete and utter fool. That I even questioned loving her made me now want to kick myself. My stupid pride and the fact that I was also just plain stupid had stopped me from telling her. She had given me the opportunity to say exactly how I felt, and I had fucked up yet again. Swallowing what vestige of idiotic pride I had left, and gathering all of my courage, I had reached out and called her a couple of times, but she hadn't answered my calls. For the first time ever, I couldn't even bring myself to tell Gabe and Eduardo what had happened, and they knew me well enough to know that this time it was serious and so they left well alone, the usual banter absent.

My mobile rang as I sat at my desk staring into space, I had been

After Paris

doing that a lot recently. I flipped it over and saw that it was Eduardo.

"Hey," I answered.

"Fuck you are never going to believe this."

"Believe what?" I asked leaning back in my chair.

"Constantine has dropped all of the charges against you."

I sat up ramrod straight. "What?"

"Yes. Can you believe it? I received the papers this morning signed by him saying all charges are dropped."

"No. I can't fucking believe that. Why would he do that?"

"I have no idea mate. But this deserves some serious celebrating."

"Holy shit."

"Tonight? Out for a drink?"

I shrugged. "Yeah ok. Why not?"

"I'll call Gabe and let him know. Would you like me to call Alyssa and let her know? It's just that I know she was so worried about you and this case."

"Yeah. Ok. It would be good coming from you. Not too sure she is worried so much now though."

"Naomi says she is."

My back straightened a bit more, my interest piqued.

"Naomi? Why have you been talking to Naomi? Is there something you want to tell me?"

Eduardo laughed. "Tonight, I will fill you in. Good news though regarding the case. Eh?"

I smiled. "Yes. I guess. Thanks Eduardo."

I clicked my phone off. I was just about to try and get down to some work when there was knock on my door and Estelle poked her head around. I waved her in. She closed the door behind her and came up to my desk. She seemed kind of nervous.

"What's up Estelle?" I asked with a smile.

"Mr. Montgomery there is a Mr. Montgomery downstairs in the lobby asking to see you."

I stared at her and for a moment I thought she was joking. But why would my hardworking, loyal assistant joke about something like that? I took a deep breath.

"Show him up Estelle please."

"Yes of course. Would you like me to bring in tea?"
"I'll check first and then yes that would be great."
I waited until she left before I let the nerves kick in.
Holy crap...my father here in my offices?
Never happened, not in the ten years or so that I had been working. My hands suddenly felt clammy, and I went into the bathroom and washed them quickly drying them before I heard the knock on my door. Estelle opened the door and entered my father followed her in. He looked as debonair as ever dressed in his Saville Row suit and brogues. He was still slim and handsome, and I could tell Estelle was completely in awe as she stood there waiting to hear if we wanted tea. I went over to him, and he held out his hand.
"Xavier. Good to see you, my boy."
I shook his hand. "Father. To what do I what this unexpected visit?" I glanced at Estelle and guessed why she was waiting expectantly by the door. "Would you like tea?"
My father nodded and turned to smile at Estelle, who blushed. He still had it - that Montgomery charm. "That would be lovely thank you."
We waited until Estelle had left before I gestured to the sofa.
"Please sit. Or would you prefer to sit around my desk?"
My father smiled. "The sofa is fine."
I nodded and sat down opposite him on the other sofa. "So, what brings you to London?"
"You Xavier. I've come to see you."
I sat back and raised my eyebrows. "If this is something to do with *maman*...."
My father shook his head. "Nope, nothing to do with your mother at all. I read the article on you in *The Aristocrat*."
I smiled. "Surprised you read that."
"I don't usually, but lots of friends and acquaintances kept asking me about it and so I thought I would give it a read...excellent article by the way. It captured you entirely accurately."
I frowned. He had no right to say that. "Sorry but how would you know?"
My father winced dramatically. "I deserved that I suppose. Contrary to what you believe, I have been keeping a close eye on

After Paris

you Xavier over the years. Sometimes I was within a hair's breadth away from you, but I kept back, and I watched, and I listened."

"But you never came forward to speak to me or ask me how I am?" My voice had gone from polite and courteous to cold and detached within minutes and I couldn't help it.

"Something I deeply regret," He replied staring straight into my eyes. "I am a stubborn man, always have been. I lost your mother because of my stubbornness, and I lost you too. I couldn't admit to being wrong and the longer I left it the harder it got to approach you."

Estelle knocked and entered with the tea and placed it on the table in front of us. She had even put some biscuits on a plate. I smiled. She only did that for people she liked.

"Thank you, Estelle. This is my father, Nicholas Montgomery. Father, this is Estelle, my very efficient and loyal assistant."

My father, always the gentleman, stood up to shake her hand and she blushed again.

"So lovely to meet you my dear."

"The pleasure is all mine. If you need anything else Mr. Montgomery just let me know."

"Thank you," I smiled.

We waited until she left before carrying on the conversation as I poured the tea.

"No milk," my father said.

I passed him his cup. "Yes, I remember."

"I remember everything about you too Xavier. You were his hero you know. Guillaume's hero."

I looked down at my tea unsure of how to respond. The mention of my brother's name made me kind of nervous of what was coming next.

"You were my first born, the love of my life. I loved you so much I found it hard to contain it sometimes. You were unruly, mischievous and a bit of a dare devil and I loved you for it. Each time that stuck up Master called me from your school threatening expulsion, I loved you even more."

I looked at him my eyes staring slightly mystified at the man in front of me. What was I hearing? That he actually loved me. Even when I thought I was being a wild, naughty tearaway, he still loved me.

"You were all the things I could ever be. My father was strict and expected me always to behave in a certain way, but you Xavier were how I wanted to be, brave and strong and wild but always trying to do the right thing. You followed your heart. Perhaps it was the French side of you from your mother that made you as you were, but I liked to think I had something to do with it too." I put my teacup down, so that my father wouldn't see my hands shaking. Fuck, this was the last thing I expected.

"So why? Why did you abandon me?" I had to ask. I needed to know.

"Because I was a fool. I was grieving, as were we all, but I blamed you unfairly for not being able to save him. His hero could not save him. But you were just a child too and really, I was blaming myself for not being there for not being able to save him. I went through years of therapy to get me to that conclusion. I suffered from depression you know for a long time afterwards. I asked your mother to keep you away. I didn't want you to see me like that. But then the time stretched, and I realised you and your mother would obviously be better off without me."

My heart plummeted at the thought of my father being alone all these years because of his stubborn pride. I wondered where I got it from and now, I knew.

"You had no right to make that decision. And you were so wrong we needed you more than ever.... *I* needed you more than ever. So, why would you think that?"

He shrugged. "Because that was where I was at in my head at the time. I know I called it wrongly. I realised that a while ago too. I should never have pushed you away, made you a scapegoat for my own issues, blaming you for a tragic accident. You were always a hero Xavier. You were my hero too you know?"

I felt actual tears prickle at the backs of my eyes. *For fuck's sake.* Not cried in twenty odd years and then in the space of a few days the tears were there at every turn wanting to flow.

"It hurt," I said my voice cracking slightly. "A lot."

My father nodded. "I know. I am sorry Xavier for causing you so much pain and hurt. I should never have done that."

After Paris

We stared at each other for a while until my father picked up his teacup and offered me a gentle smile.
"I would like to get to know the man you have become, which is a good, honest, hardworking, and generous man according to that young woman who wrote the article. Do you think we can see each other now and then?"
I smiled back. "I would love to see you. Get to know you again. There's a lot happened over the years. Perhaps I can come and see you in Hampshire?"
My father nodded as he drank his tea. "I shall look forward to it."
"I may bring someone with me…that same young woman who wrote the article."
"I would be honoured. Is there something between you and her? Maybe I am wrong but reading between the lines…"
"I love her," I said surprising myself with how easily that came out. "But I have let her go, pushed her away. Seems you and I have more in common than you thought."
My father smiled warmly. "Then I suggest you go after her Xavier and then hang onto her tightly. Don't make the same mistakes I did. It's too late for me but not for you."
"It's not too late. We're here and we're talking." My voice croaked a bit with emotion.
My father looked at me for a long moment, a sad smile upon his lips and then put his teacup on the table. We stood up together and walked to the door.
"Thank you for seeing me today," my father said as I reached to open the door. "I wasn't sure you would after so long. But you are a good man. I am so proud of that fact."
"Thank you for coming. It has been good to talk."
"We have a lot of talking to do my boy, so don't wait too long before coming to see me."
We shook hands and then I did something totally impulsive and pulled him into a hug and all those lost years almost fell away. When we pulled apart, he smiled and leaned towards me.
"Oh, by the way, Constantine will never bother you again. I have made sure of that. If you have any further hassle with him, please let me know and I will punch him myself," He whispered close

to my ear.

My mouth fell open in surprise as I watched him say goodbye to Estelle and make his way to the lift.

Fuck me. Sometimes life is just full of surprises.

CHAPTER TWENTY-TWO

Alyssa

"Please, please, please come tonight," Naomi begged. "I have made you a dress especially."
"What? No, you haven't. You are just trying to bribe me to come out for a drink when you know I am not going to go because a certain person will be there," I glared at her.
Naomi sighed loudly. "Oh, for God's sake Alyssa. Of course, he will be there. They are celebrating him being let off charges for punching your dick head ex-fiancé; surely you should come for that last fact alone."
I didn't know how it had happened, but I was so glad Xavier was now not going to have to defend himself in court against Theo.
"I do not want to see him," I dug my heels in. Oh yes, I could be stubborn when I wanted to be.
"He is missing you like crazy. Eduardo says Xavier is beside himself."
I looked at her, an unwavering stare that made her blush.
"What?" she finally said.
I raised my eyebrows. "Eduardo?"
She shrugged. "We have been out a few times. Nothing serious. Casual. You know…?"
I shook my head. "No. I don't know. I thought you didn't do casual?"

"For a man like Eduardo Espinosa you kind of have to make compromises."

My mouth fell open in mock horror. "What? Ok where is my friend Naomi? Who the hell are you?"

Her grin spread and so did mine and soon we were both laughing. "Have you slept with him?" I asked widening my eyes in jest, wriggling my eyebrows.

She snorted and then laughed. "No. I haven't but it is so damned hard not to. I really want to, but I don't want to be just another one of his women. Do you know what I mean?"

"You're asking me that?" I laugh. "Please. Been there and got the t-shirt."

She smiled. "Oh yes sorry."

"Turned out I *was* just another one of his women."

Naomi turned serious. "Not true. I saw the way he looked at you. He loves you but he's just in denial."

"Yes well. He was pretty good with the denying part. He has totally convinced me."

"Please come tonight. Your book has been submitted to the publishers finally, so we also have something to celebrate."

I thought about it. I was aching to see Xavier, but I was also hurting. Could I suffer being humiliated in front of our friends too? I shook my head.

"Sorry Naomi. You go and have a nice time. I am too upset to see him now."

She sighed again but I could tell she wouldn't push it anymore. We knew each other well enough to know when to give up.

"I think you're mad but ok. I get it," She smiled at me sadly.

I gave her a hug and she hugged me back. It was going to kill me not to go tonight but my stubbornness had kicked in and I never backed down when it did.

I knew that I was asking too much of Xavier. It wasn't his fault that I loved him. I just did. Nothing I could do about it. It had hurt when he tried to let me down gently. I would rather he had just laughed in my face, at least then I would have had a chance of getting over him, of moving on. Over this past week I had thought over and over if maybe I had said it too early, but it came

After Paris

straight from the heart and now I couldn't take it back. I didn't want to take it back. I loved him but he didn't love me, couldn't love me. He even said he didn't know if he could ever love me. I had pushed him too hard; I knew his background and still I expected him to fall head over heels in love with me in five minutes flat, just like I had him. My heart ached for him; I missed him so much it hurt. I wasn't aware that I was crying until a tear slid down my cheek and splashed on the back of my hand, just when I thought I had no tears left. I grabbed a tissue from the box that had been by my side for the past seven days and wiped my face. Wistfully I thought about the guys and Naomi having a celebration without me and this made me even more sad. I am such a drama queen sometimes. Why couldn't I have just gone with Naomi and swallowed my stupid pride. Because I am an idiot that's why and I deserve to be sitting in alone and feeling sorry for myself. Time for bath and a Netflix film - and copious amounts of Ben & Jerry's ice cream and a glass of wine to wash it all down.

I had a wonderful bath and then put on my old comfy pyjamas and got myself a big glass of wine. Pouilly Fumé. Turned out I liked French wine almost as much as I liked French men. I looked on Netflix to see what was on and found a film that looked good. I was just about to click it on when there was a ring at the door. If that was Naomi come to convince me she was going to be severely disappointed. I was not going out to meet Xavier and his friends.
I looked through the spyhole. Oh. My. Fuck. It was Xavier. I jumped back shocked, and he rang the bell again. I looked at him through the spyhole and although a bit distorted, he looked divine. He was dressed in a black suit and a white shirt open at the neck, my favourite look on him and his hair was all wild and unruly, just like I liked it and I watched as he pushed it back nervously from his forehead as he waited for me to open the door.
Shit. Here goes. I took a deep breath and threw the door open.
"Xavier," I smiled. "What are you doing here?"
Without saying a word, he pushed me back in through the door

and closed it behind him.

"Why don't you come in?" I said trying to ignore the fact that he smelt as good as he looked.

"You didn't come to celebrate," he said in an accusing tone.

"I told Naomi to buy you a drink from me."

"I don't want a drink from you. I want you," He stared at me and then did that thing that drove me crazy. He looked at my mouth like he wanted to devour it and I cleared my throat nervously.

"What are you saying? Are you drunk?"

"Fuck no. I am not drunk. I am saying that I want you. Do you need me to say it in French before you understand?"

I shook my head. I didn't want him to say anything in French because that would be the end. I had no resistance at all to him speaking in French. "If you mean sexually…well I think you have a bloody nerve coming here…."

"For fuck's sake Alyssa, I love you. I love you."

I stared at him rolling my lips together trying to piece together what he had just said to me.

He stared back at me as the silence stretched "Ok. I am going in with the French too. *Je t'aime* Alyssa. *Je suis amoureux de toi.* I am in love with you."

He took me gently by the upper arms and pulled me towards him. Before I swooned, I had to ask him. "Do you want to run that by me one more time in French?"

He shook his head and hid a smile that was tugging at his beautiful full lips.

"*Je t'aime* Alyssa James."

"I love you too," I whispered back.

"Yes, I know. You told me and I acted like an idiot. I am sorry."

I pushed him away from me reluctantly. "You need to explain more than that Xavier. You hurt me."

His blue eyes stared into mine, full of emotions that I had never seen before. Regret, sadness and maybe a touch of humility too.

"Alyssa, I loved you when I didn't even know you. I loved you when I sat down at that table at the café in Paris that day. I loved you when we had that night of passion, and I didn't even know it was you. I loved you every time you tried to resist me. But the thing is I didn't want to admit that I was capable of feeling love.

After Paris

My internal barriers went up when I was thirteen and stayed firmly in place and until you came along and began to chip away at them. But it was hard to let the old me go; it was all I knew for a long time. But you are too good to let go Alyssa James. You have made me the man that now stands before you. You said that I couldn't be the man you would want to love you…. but guess what? You don't have a choice and neither do I. *Je t'aime* Alyssa."
I stared at him my eyes welling with tears. "OMG, that was the best thing that anyone has ever said to me."
He grinned. "And I meant every word. I have really missed you."
I put my arms around his neck and pulled him towards me. "I have missed you too. So much."
"Yeah?" he pushed me up against the wall in the hallway.
I nodded, taking his beautiful face in my hands and kissing him. He kissed me back and I groaned.
He pulled away from me grinning. "Will you stop groaning like that?" he laughed and kissed me again.
"Can't help it," I murmured in between kisses.
"Mmmmh," he said with his lip grazing over my cheek. "Forgot to tell you something."
"Right now?" I asked revelling in his kisses and running my hands down his back to his very pert round hard buttocks. He pulled his lips away from my neck.
"My father came to see me," he said gently looking straight into my eyes. "He read your article, and it gave him the courage to finally make that decision. He wanted to meet the man that you wrote about so eloquently."
I was both amazed and overcome with emotion at the same time. This time the tears came in full, sliding silently down my cheeks. Xavier smiled and lovingly wiped them away with his thumb pad.
"Seriously?" I whispered between tears. "He came to see you? You actually talked?"
Xavier nodded. "So, in a way you brought us back together. He wants to meet you by the way."
"You told him about me?"
"Of course I did. I'll tell you everything later but right now there are other more pressing things on my mind." He pulled me to him so that I could feel exactly what he was talking about.

"You still fancy me even in this outfit?" I smirked.

He looked at my pyjamas and rolled his eyes. "What the fuck are these? I really cannot have my girlfriend going around in this type of attire."

I laughed. "Listen Mr. Casanova, the goods are the same underneath, ok?"

"When we're married, I am going to make sure that you never wear these again."

"Do you know what? I am going to always wear exactly...." I stopped suddenly. "What did you just say?"

"That when we are married these pyjamas are banned…in fact you won't need pyjamas ever again."

I narrowed eyes at him. "Married?"

He nodded. "Yes. Married. Want me to say it in French?"

I shook my head. "Oh my God, you can say that in any language you like."

"Do you want to marry me, Alyssa?"

I opened my mouth and then closed it again.

He raised his eyebrows. "Well?"

"How do you say, 'I'll think about it' in French?"

He pulled me to him and crushed his lips against mine and it felt so good, and it felt so right.

"You say one word," he whispered against my lips. "*Oui.*"

The End or is it the beginning....

HOPE YOU ENJOYED THIS BOOK

PLEASE LOOK OUT FOR THE NEXT TWO BOOKS IN THE SERIES

"AFTER THE WEDDING" EDUARDO AND NAOMI'S STORY SPRING 2025

AND

"AFTER FOREVER" GABE AND SOFIA'S STORY AUTUMN 2025

ABOUT THE AUTHOR

Hi Everyone

My name is Jacqueline Bacci. I am married with one son and live in the beautiful county of Essex, just outside of London.

I started writing books many moons ago, whilst still at school, and I have an old chest upstairs in my house filled with dozens of handwritten manuscripts. My writing was for my own pleasure, and I lost myself for hours in the love lives of the couples who only existed in my head and my heart. If I was a piece of seaside rock, I would have the word 'romance' written right through me.

I lived in Florence Italy for a few years in my twenties as I longed to learn the Italian language and I came away with a passion for everything Italian (plus an Italian husband!)

My books are about love and sizzling passion and couples who overcome every obstacle to be together and there is always a happy ever after.

After everything, love conquers all.